HIDDEN CITY

By
CHESTER S. GEIER

ARMCHAIR FICTION
PO Box 4369, Medford, Oregon 97504

A DEADLY RACE FOR THE MOON...

Two men were scheduled to make history. They were going to be the first to rocket into space and make a landing on the Moon. But that was only going to happen if they were able to launch in secrecy. Danger before and during launch was expected. Others, in league to stop them, formed a formidable organization intent on sabotage and murder.

Harvey Dall and Jules Frontenac were space pioneers. The first to finish a rocket, the first to take off, and maybe the first to never return. What they found on the surface of the Moon would astound even the most educated and hopeful men of science. There, beneath the surface of the moon, was an amazing city...

CAST OF CHARACTERS

HARVEY DALL
Designer of the first functioning rocket ship, he had a lot of obstacles to overcome. Would he even get the chance board it?

JULES FRONTENAC
He was the "money man" for this rocket set-up and nothing was going to stop him from getting to the Moon.

BRUCE MELGARD
As head mechanic he had open access to the project field. His goal? To put a stop to all progress…now.

ELLEN PANCREST
As intriguing a girl as ever was, she called herself the Phrenarch of Lunapolis—and she was going to conquer the world.

MAJOR RANKIN
Shaken by his commanding officer's faulty thinking, he would soon realize he was a better soldier for the other side.

LLOYD PANCREST
Founder of a new society of men and women who were smarter, faster, stronger than the average human: "The Neo-man."

JONOTHAN
A relic of the once great city called Lunapolis, his job was to protect all life and its evolutionary process.

CHAPTER ONE

IT WAS all too familiar, that sensation of dark unease. Dall had never failed to experience it on his occasional visits to the city during the last several months. But this time—knowing that the work was over, that he and Frontenac were ready to leave at last—it was sharper, more penetrating.

He pulled the brim of his hat low over wary, metal-gray eyes and leaned against the waist-high mahogany counter behind him in an effort to conceal his raw-boned, towering height. He was acutely aware of the neon sign overhead, spelling out the words *Parking Agent.* Too bright that sign; too eye-attracting. A growing impatience underscored his feeling of disquiet.

His vigilant gaze probed the ceaseless ebb and flow of the human tide that filled the airport terminal building. A kaleidoscope of bobbing faces and hurrying forms against a background of blazing lights and constantly shifting colors. The voices of the crowd mingled in a confused babble, rising and falling in pitch. From outside the building came the drone and thunder of aircraft, taking off or arriving at the vast field. And at intervals, stabbing through the uproar, came the booming tones of the flight announcer over the radio system.

To the casual observer, the scene would have been one of intense interest. But to Dall it held a threat of danger. Secrecy had shrouded his departure from the construction camp in northern Michigan, but he knew that his absence might already be noticed; that word of his going might already be sent to the various points that would most logically be among his destination. He didn't know who, among the mechanics and technical staff still remaining at the camp, was the spy that would sound the alert, but he was certain that an alert would be sounded.

He touched the flat automatic nestling in a hip pocket of his flannel suit, and the lines of his bronzed, spare face deepened with momentary grimness. *They* knew he was here—and they would be planning to prevent Frontenac and him from taking off in the ship. They might strike in the very midst of the crowd. They—if the things that had happened within the past few years actually meant such an organization existed—were devilishly cunning and audacious. They had to be, to have succeeded so well thus far in their subtle, half-sensed designs, without having betrayed more than a hint of their presence and purpose.

AGAIN those questions nagged in Dall's mind. Just who were *They?* Just why were they blocking, through murder and sabotage, all efforts to conquer space?

"Here you are, sir," a voice behind Dall said. He turned as a girl clerk behind the mahogany counter extended a small oblong of colored pasteboard. It was the parking receipt for his private flitterjet; he took it, nodding briskly to cover up the startled jerk with which he had responded to her words.

The girl was more than ordinarily attractive, and her smile at Dall contained more than the usual amount of courtesy that the girl clerks at the terminal customarily bestowed upon parking patrons. But Dall, slipping the receipt into a pocket of his jacket, was too preoccupied to notice. He glanced up at the huge clock on the wall beyond the counter, figuring rapidly. There would be just enough time to pick up the spare, special injectors Frontenac had ordered, keep the appointment with his, Dall's lawyer, and be on the way back to camp in time to avoid the after-work rush of craft bearing workers from the city to their homes in outlying suburbs. The lawyer detail wasn't absolutely necessary, but Dall couldn't be certain that he and Frontenac would return safely from their trial flight to the Moon. If they didn't, a will would be very much in order. The money involved was far from being a fortune, but he felt the least he could do was to leave it to people to whom it would be of use.

"Can I help you in any way?" the girl asked. She smiled again, and lifted a slim hand to tuck away a few stray tendrils of the blonde hair arranged in gleaming coils atop her shapely head.

Dall grinned briefly, teeth flashing white against the bronze of his skin. "No, thanks." He turned and slipped into the maelstrom of the crowd, dodging and elbowing his way toward a group of revolving doors that gave out to the taxi stands.

The blonde clerk gazed wistfully after him a moment, sighed, and then turned to resume her work.

Dall stopped at a newsstand near the doors to buy a paper. He had resumed his progress, glancing over the headlines, when he abruptly became aware that two men had fallen into step with him, one on either side. He froze into motionlessness, cursing himself for having failed to maintain his guard.

"Are you Harvey Dall?" one of the men asked.

Dall said nothing. He surveyed his questioner carefully, then glanced at the other's companion. Both were young men, average in height and features, and neatly but unobtrusively dressed. The only thing striking or at all unusual about them was their eyes; steady eyes, penetrating, vigorously and intelligently alert.

Dall said slowly, "Just what do you want?"

"I'll take the question as an admission that you're Harvey Dall," the man who had first spoken said. "We want you to come along with us, Mr. Dall. We'll explain when we reach a place with more privacy."

DALL had been expecting an attack, but he hadn't guessed it would happen as naively as this. He smiled grimly—a smile that didn't move his lips. Did *They* think he was a fool? He shrugged, nodded as though in agreement at his two accosters, and started once more for the revolving doors. His long legs kept him easily in the lead, despite the efforts of the men to remain at his side.

Near the doors, Dall suddenly darted around the plump figure of an entering woman, ducking into the compartment that she had just left. The two men immediately sprang after him, both crowding into the next compartment in their haste.

Dall's next action was made with blurred swiftness. As his compartment swung outside, he whirled, throwing his weight against the panel behind him. The two men, on the other side, were taken completely by surprise. Before they could recover and resist his push, Dall wedged the newspaper he had bought firmly between the top of the panel and the ceiling above. It took strength to do it at all; Dall had plenty of that, and he used every erg of it. When he finally hurried away, it was to leave the two momentarily imprisoned within the triangular space formed by the compartment panels and the concave wall behind. It would take some seconds—if not actual minutes—for them to push free and Dall hoped to be well on his way by that time.

The whole thing had happened fast, covering mere instants. Dall had reached a taxi and was ducking inside before the first cries and shouts of alarm rose from behind, at the doors.

"Take me to the Loop," he told the driver. "And quick. There's a ten in it for you, if you're fast."

The man hesitated. "What happened back there?"

"Couple of men got stuck in a revolving door. They were right behind me, and I'd rather not get dragged in as an accident witness. Time is money to me. Remember that ten, will you?"

"I don't aim to forget, mister." The cabbie straightened in his seat and stamped the car into motion.

As they moved with gathering speed down the driveway, toward the exit gates of the terminal, Dall turned in his seat to peer through the rear window. There was a crowd about the revolving doors. He decided, with bleak satisfaction that the two men were still boxed in. Then, as he glanced at the figures standing near the spot where he had entered the taxi, seeking signs of pursuit, his eyes narrowed in sudden, intense interest. For among the persons staring after the cab was a tall, slender man, with a flowing mane of snow-white hair. He was hatless, dressed in a conservative dark suit. Across the rapidly widening chasm placed between them by the accelerating cab, Dall could discern only hazy details of the other's face; but he knew, from data still fresh in his memory that it was a long, slim face, utterly smooth, with a pale, ascetic quality that suggested the secluded, austere life of one devoted to religion or to science. That tall form, with its mop of white hair, had been all Dall needed for a complete picture of the man.

THE taxi rounded a turn in the driveway, and Dall's view was abruptly cut off. He straightened and peered unseeingly ahead, frowning in amazed thought. It had happened a little over two weeks ago, he remembered, near evening. There had been a lull in the work at the camp, and he had taken a walk in the forest a short distance away. Turning a bend in the narrow path that he had been following, he had come suddenly upon the tall, white-haired man.

They had gazed at each other across a gap of less than twenty feet, Dall staring in surprise, the stranger calm and impassive, oddly aloof. Not a word had been uttered. Dall hadn't been able to find anything to say, as he'd looked into eyes that held his with a fixity verging on the hypnotic; dark eyes, steady and intense that seemed bottomless pools of wisdom, reflecting in their depths the flame of a mind that burned with a brilliance, transcending the human—supernal, god-like.

Dall had a curious sense of unreality regarding the time that had passed while his and the stranger's glances had remained locked. Mere seconds, certainly, yet they had seemed like years. He had felt frozen, numbed. And there was the disturbing impression that somehow his mind had been searched, scanned as one scans the pages of a book in quest of pertinent information.

And then the white-haired stranger had gone—vanished completely. He had turned suddenly, striding off the path; trees and underbrush had concealed him from sight; and when, scant instants later, Dall had shaken free of his paralysis and raced after in pursuit, he had found nothing. No sound had broken the deep stillness of the forest—no patter of running feet, no roar of a departing flitterjet. Yet the man had been nowhere to be seen.

Now, at the airport, he had encountered the stranger again. It was more than coincidence, Dall was certain. But what was the man doing at the airport? And for that matter, what had he been doing near the camp two weeks before? Who—or *what*— was he? Was he connected with that mysterious and practically mythical group Dall knew only as *They*?

Dall thought abruptly of the two men who had accosted him within the terminal. How did they fit in? Were they and the white-haired man in league? It seemed a likely guess; for the three to have been in the same place, at the same time, could have been no coincidence, either.

The taxi reached the Drive, and nosed its way into a growing stream of Loop-bound surface traffic. Dall peered once more through the rear window, but the dense mass of cars that had by now closed in behind made it impossible to tell if he had been followed. The cabbie, however, was earning his bonus. With deft and often breathtaking skill, he sent the car weaving and darting through the maze of machines ahead, rapidly increasing the distance between them.

The Loop was situated several blocks from the lake-front air terminal, and the cabbie reached it in record time, considering the amount of vehicular traffic in that part of the city. Dall paid the fare, adding the money he had promised, and left the taxi. He walked quickly up one street, down another, and then for good measure cut through a busy department store, to emerge shortly on still another street. A taxi with its flag up cruised past; he hailed it and gave the address of a small near North side factory that did special aircraft work.

A little over an hour later, with a small fibre box containing the spare injectors now in his possession, Dall appeared at the office of his lawyer. The details of the will were rapidly concluded. Rising to leave, Dall paused under the impulse of a sudden idea. He sat down again and rapidly sketched his encounter with the two men back at the terminal. Bonfield could be trusted, he knew; the lawyer was an old friend, had handled numerous patents for Dall, and had not long since won a lawsuit involving one of Dall's inventions.

"The two will most likely be waiting at the terminal for me to return," Dall finished. "They won't be taken in so easily a second time, and I'd rather not play any more games. Could you send someone to pick up my ship and deliver it to me at some field in another part of the town?"

BONFIELD nodded without hesitation. "Can do, Harv. I know just the man—a private dick named Curtis. He's worked on a lot of ticklish jobs for me, and he's just what you need. But it'll cost you."

"Hang the cost," Dall grunted. "I want to get out of the city with as little fuss as possible."

Bonfield turned to the visiphone cabinet on his desk and dialed a number. He spoke quickly to the sharp-faced man who presently appeared in the screen. Arrangements were soon concluded: Dall was to leave with Bonfield the parking receipt for his flitterjet; Curtis would come to pick it up; then, obtaining the craft, he would fly it to the small Uptown terminal, where Dall would be waiting.

Satisfied, Dall rose again, extending a lean, brown hand. "The *Frontier* takes off the day after tomorrow, Jim. In case Frontenac and I don't get back, this is so-long. Period."

The lawyer rose, too, gripping Dall's hand. He smiled quietly. "If I know you, Harv, you'll get back."

A few minutes later Dall was down in the street. Locating another taxi, he ordered himself driven to the Uptown terminal.

He arrived at his destination within a quarter of an hour. With a lighted cigarette to ease the strain of waiting, he strolled along the margin of the field, watching the sky. A large number of flitterjets landed, but it wasn't until he had started on a second cigarette that one finally appeared with a license number that he identified as his own. He hurried across to the spot where it landed.

Curtis had already climbed from the cabin when Dall came up. The private detective was a small, thin man in a rumpled, dark suit.

"Sure you weren't followed?" Dall asked.

Curtis' eyes shifted in a way that to Dall seemed oddly evasive. "I watched, Mr. Dall. There was no ship behind me all the way up here."

"Good." Dall shrugged mentally at the impression that the other had given him, deciding he had misinterpreted it. He produced his wallet and extracted a bill. "Here's your fee for the job, Curtis."

The detective drew back. "I don't want your money, Mr. Dall."

And as Dall stared in bewilderment, the other abruptly turned and hurried away. He was gone from sight before thought of pursuit entered Dall's dazed mind. Shrugging, then, with a mixture of irritation and disgust, Dall replaced his wallet and climbed into the flitterjet.

Two men rose from sight in the club seat at the rear of the craft, evidently having previously been keeping themselves doubled up in hiding. They were the same men from whom Dall had escaped at the Loop terminal. One of them held a gun; he pointed it at Dall and said:

"No more tricks, please."

CHAPTER TWO

FOR long seconds an icy dismay held Dall petrified. Fool, he thought, blind fool! How could he have been so stupid as to have missed the warning that had been in Curtis' strange actions?

Then his mind accepted the situation for the irrevocable thing it was. He slowly sat down in the pilot seat, aware that the gun vigilantly followed his move. He looked at the alert faces opposite him and lifted his wide shoulders in a shrug.

"All right, you've got me. What now?"

"Take a look at this, Mr. Dall." It was the unarmed man who had spoken. He produced a plain envelope from an inner pocket of his suit, ripped it open, and extended a folded sheet of paper that seemed curiously thick.

Wary, a trifle bewildered, Dall took it. The sheet, he found, bore the letterhead of the United States Secret Service, and was addressed to him. Photographs of the two men were attached to the sheet; a few sentences of typewritten text introduced them, explaining who they were, and requested that Dall co-operate with them in every way. Beneath a little-known signature was the Great Seal of the United States.

Dall stared incredulously at the two. He exclaimed, with involuntary softness, "Secret Service agents!"

The man who had given Dall the letter of introduction nodded quietly. "We could have given you that information back at the Loop terminal, if you had given us the chance, Mr. Dall."

Dall said slowly, "That's all very well, George Metz—if that's actually your name—but how can I be certain this letter isn't a clever forgery?"

Metz' answering smile came easily. "Well, Mr. Dall, agents like Tom Bushnell and myself don't ordinarily carry letters of identification; they have other means of making themselves known. Identification like this is carried only when the usual means would be just so much mumbo-mumbo; and when it is carried, ample provision against forgery or fraudulent use is made in the event that it is lost or stolen.

"You noticed, for example, that I opened the envelope instead of letting you do that yourself? Well, opening it by any other method than the one I used would cause the thing to explode instantly into flames. And as for the letter itself"— Metz' voice was suddenly sharp and commanding—"wad it up, Mr. Dall, and throw it as far from the plane as you can!"

There was something about the other's tone that decided Dall not to hesitate. Hastily squeezing the letter into a shapeless mass, he tossed it through the open door of the cabin. He saw it hit and roll to a stop on the hard-packed earth of the field; saw it, instants later, burst abruptly into fire and burn down to a few thin gray ashes, which were caught up by the breeze and scattered beyond reclaim.

Metz chuckled softly. "Convinced, Mr. Dall?"

"It could still be a trick," Dall grunted, glancing at Bushnell's gun.

BUSHNELL smiled and slid the weapon into his coat. "Suppose you take a chance on us? This isn't an arrest, you know; you're just being asked to co-operate."

"All right, I'll stick my neck out," Dall said. "What do you want me to do?"

"We want you to come with us to a certain place," Metz answered. "Your ship will be OK. We could guide you there, but it might save time if you let one of us take over."

Dall nodded; Bushnell volunteered to pilot the flitterjet, and Dall exchanged seats with him. Shortly, with a roar of its whirling overhead jets, the craft took off, heading north.

After several minutes of thoughtful silence, Dall glanced at Metz, who reclined quietly at his side. He asked, "How did you get out of those revolving doors back at the Loop terminal?"

Metz' grin held a touch of wryness. "An employee folded back a couple of the panels behind us, so that we could get back into the building. That front panel was stuck fast. Quick thinking on your part, Mr. Dall; by the time we got outside, you were already out of sight. Since we knew it would be useless to follow, we decided to wait for you in your ship. The blonde clerk gave us the number of your parking space; she'd remembered it for some reason. As to how we got inside...well, that's one of the first things we learn, Mr. Dall."

"Curtis found out you two were inside?"

"The little man with the hatchet face? Yes—first thing he did. But we identified ourselves and told him to take the ship to wherever he was supposed to deliver it. He seemed too impressed to think of doing anything else."

"You and Bushnell were alone?"

"Alone, Mr. Dall."

"There wasn't a tall man with thick white hair along with you?"

"No. Why do you ask?"

"Just an idea I had," Dall said. "By the way, how did you find out that I was going to show up at the Loop terminal?"

Metz grinned slightly, and shrugged. "Trade secret, Mr. Dall."

"A little spy told you, eh?" Dall persisted. "I had reason to believe there was a spy back at camp, but I never guessed the Secret Service was involved."

Metz said, somewhat cryptically, "We'll talk about that later. We're almost there."

The flitterjet had been following the shoreline along the Lake, traveling at top speed. Now it swung inland and toward the west. Watching through the window at his side, Dall saw a small, neat suburb appear below. Their destination seemed to be some point there, for Bushnell cut speed and sent the ship angling down. Shortly Dall realized that they were dropping toward a large, walled-in estate on the suburb's outskirts. The place, as he gradually made out details, seemed abandoned: grass and weeds grew thickly on the grounds, and the huge brick house squatting in their midst showed clearly evident signs of disrepair.

TWO large, luxury-model flitterjets rested on the ground near the house. Bushnell landed a short distance away; and Dall followed as Bushnell and then Metz climbed out.

Metz gazed toward the house a moment, then waved his arms in what was obviously a signal. He gestured to Dall, grinned briefly, and said, "That's so we wouldn't be put to the inconvenience of picking machine gun slugs out of our carcasses."

The door was opened by a man not much different physically or facially from Metz or Bushnell. With a nod at the two and a searching glance at Dall, he jerked a thumb toward a large doorway to the right of the hall they had entered. "Chief's in there," he said.

The room beyond was huge, filled with dusty, long-outmoded furniture. A group consisting of seven men was present. Most of these held machine guns and stood about the edges of the room, near the windows. Two were seated at a table in the middle of the room: one was slight, gray-haired, dressed in a plain gray suit; the other, heavier, ruddy-faced, and also gray-haired, wore an army uniform with the stars of a general.

Metz and Bushnell, with Dall following in growing perplexity, advanced toward the table and saluted. The two men seated there rose as Dall was introduced. The man in civilian clothes, he learned, was John Merrick, chief of the United States Secret Service. Dall recalled Merrick's signature as having been on the letter that Metz had given him. The uniformed man was General Stuart Weston, head of Army Intelligence.

Dall's confusion mounted. What did all this mean? Why had he been brought here, before these important men?

Merrick gestured to a chair at the table, and Dall, moving with unaccustomed stiffness, joined him and Weston in sitting down. Metz and Bushnell remained standing. Merrick turned his attention to them and asked:

"Reports?"

Metz glanced inquiringly at his partner, and Bushnell nodded. Assuming the role of spokesman, Metz economically detailed the sequence of events starting with his and Bushnell's accosting of Dall at the Loop terminal and ending with the incident at the Uptown field. He left nothing out. Merrick and Weston glanced at each other at a couple of points in the recital, and once, when Metz related the episode of the revolving doors, they smiled.

METZ and Bushnell, their job done, retired to a corner of the room. Merrick turned to Dall.

"No doubt you're wondering why General Weston and I are here, Mr. Dall, and why you've been brought to us in such a roundabout way. I shall explain. But first it might be best if I gave a rough sketch of certain facts.

"As a well-known rocket engineer and authority on rockets in general, you are, of course, fully aware of the progress in rocketry that has been made up to the present. Beginning with the first jet-propelled planes and giant rocket bombs, scientific and technical knowledge has advanced to the point where penetration of interplanetary space by man-carrying rockets is now a distinct possibility. We already have in widespread commercial operation stratosphere rocket craft, which from a mechanical and structural viewpoint, are theoretically capable of leaving the earth.

"You are also aware that numerous groups, private and government sponsored, are in feverish competition with each other to be first in launching a passenger rocket into space. You represent one of them, Mr. Dall. You are thus in a position to bear me out when I say that the problems confronting these groups can hardly be termed difficult; most of the major research has already been completed. Prototypes of space rockets—stratosphere rocket craft—are already in operation. It is merely a question of more powerful, compact fuels, stronger, more efficient engines. The biggest obstacle is money, but in most cases it is being liberally supplied by various sources: large corporations, wealthy individuals, universities, and even by the government itself."

Merrick leaned forward; his voice lowered, slowed. "What makes the situation completely incredible is that, despite all this technical knowledge and financial encouragement, no experimenter has yet succeeded. And why? Mainly because of what may be termed unfortunate happenings. Rockets have blown up in tests without ever having left the ground; others have exploded shortly after taking off, killing their crews; and experimenters have died in the midst of their work, taking with them jealously kept secrets that prevented others from carrying on. In all cases the deaths have apparently been due to accidents or natural causes—but the very frequency of them, among a certain type of men, suggests that they might really be murder. And the rocket accidents, in turn, might not be accidents at all, but deliberate, planned sabotage."

DALL nodded gravely. "Speaking from a personal experience of my own, I am convinced that's just what they are. You see, the rocket that Jules Frontenac and I have built— through funds supplied by Frontenac, incidentally—isn't the first I've worked on. There was one before it that blew up in a radio-controlled ground test. I lost every cent I had at the time. The test was just routine; both before and after, I'm positive that the rocket had no mechanical flaws. The only explanation for the blast is that the ship was tampered with in some way."

"Then I need hint no longer, Mr. Dall," Merrick stated, his features suddenly grim and intent. "I'll come right out and say that General Weston and I are certain that it actually is murder and sabotage. That is why we are here. We believe that some hidden, powerful group is working desperately, using every fiendishly cunning means at their disposal, to stop rocket research not only in this country, but in other countries as well. Fully authenticated reports show that every nation engaged in space rocket research has had its share of accidents and deaths. This thing is on a worldwide scale, and as such it would seem that the idea is not so much to stop space rocket research, but to prevent men from conquering space. Now why should this be, Mr. Dall? What can possibly be the reason behind it? Why should any group want to prevent men from going beyond the earth?"

Weston joined in for the first time. "Look at it this way, Mr. Dall. What interplanetary body is the goal of practically all rocket researchers?"

"The Moon," Dall returned unhesitatingly. "Until it is shown that a trip to and from the Moon can be made successfully, it would be sheer suicide to go anywhere further away."

Weston nodded. "The Moon—exactly! Is it thus too far-fetched to suppose that the object of this mysterious group, in sabotaging rocket research, is not merely to prevent men from conquering space—but actually to prevent them from reaching the Moon? Is there something on the Moon that this group desires to keep undiscovered?"

Dall stared in amazement at Weston. A protest stirred in his mind, but he said nothing.

Weston met Dall's gaze imperturbably, smiling slightly. "I realize, of course, how fantastic this guess is. The Moon to all appearance is a dead world; airless, uninhabited, and as far as we know as yet unreached by man. But Merrick and I have discussed the possibility at some length—so often, in fact, that it no longer seems incredible to us. After all, there would be little or no reason to keep man earthbound, unless it were to prevent him from reaching some objective beyond the earth, the Moon being the most immediate. Is it thus too extreme to suppose that there is something on the Moon that an unknown group is seeking, for some reason, to keep from being found?"

MERRICK tapped the table in an emphatic gesture. "And that, Mr. Dall, leads us to the reason why you've been brought here. If there actually is something on the Moon, the worldwide efforts that have been made to keep us in ignorance about it mean it is extremely important that we learn what it is. The welfare of our nation and of the world may depend on it.

"But, Mr. Dall"—Merrick tapped the table again—"you are the only man on earth who at present is capable of acquiring this information. Your work has progressed without interference to the point where you are ready to leave earth. I have been informed of the battle that you have fought—successfully, thus far—to keep your rocket from being destroyed like all the others. The battle is by no means over yet—but somehow you must win out; somehow you must reach the Moon and obtain the information we need."

Dall nodded slowly, with grimly quiet determination. "I'll do my best, sir."

"I knew I could count on you," Merrick said softly. He rose and Weston, as though taking a cue, rose also. Merrick smiled and went on, "You will be doing your country a great service, Mr. Dall. And the world as well. In return for your courage and loyalty, will you accept, as a token of appreciation from our government, the title of Special Operative of the United States Secret Service?"

Dall jerked to his feet. "Accept? Why, it would be impossible to refuse!"

"Then lift your right hand, Harvey Dall, and repeat after me the following oath: *I do solemnly swear...*"

Awe-inspiring words, slowly and impressively spoken. Dall felt a strange chill as he repeated them, and an unaccustomed tightness clutched at his throat. For behind those words was more than a man named John Merrick, more than a little-known government agency called the Secret Service; behind them was a nation whose deeds in every field of human endeavor had placed it in the very forefront of the greatest powers of the world.

Finally it was over—Dall had taken the oath. And he knew at that moment it was one that he would not forget easily or lightly, cast aside. It bound him just as securely as chains of the strongest steel; it was something that would be a part of him always.

From a pocket of his coat Merrick produced a slim black case and snapped it open. He lifted into sight a plain platinum wristwatch and extended it to Dall.

"This is your badge of identification, Special Operative Dall. You will notice what seems to be a thin line of decorative engraving around the sides of the case. This is actually a microscopic code, containing such details as your name, title, height, weight, and other items of physical description, together with your fingerprint formulas, and a perfect though extremely tiny copy of your own signature."

Dall shook his head in wonder. "It seems impossible that you could have learned all that."

"We of the Secret Service have our methods," Merrick returned, with a brief smile. "There is no time to explain them just now; you must listen carefully to the instructions that I am going to give you."

Merrick spoke slowly and distinctly. Dall learned how to contact the main office, how to locate other operatives, how to use certain emergency signs and passwords, and other immediately necessary details of his new position. Then Dall found himself shaking hands with Merrick and Weston, and a moment later with Metz and Bushnell, who had come forward to offer their congratulations.

Merrick became brusque. "I hardly need remind you, Special Operative Dall, that the hopes of the United States and of the other nations of the world go with you on your mission. You will be fighting a clever and powerful foe, who will make every effort to prevent you from carrying it out. As far as is humanly possible, you must not fail. That is all; you are dismissed. Carry on—and good luck."

Dall saluted as he had seen Metz and Bushnell salute. Then he turned and strode swiftly from the room, lines etching the corners of his mouth and eyes; lines that had not been there before...

CHAPTER THREE

THE lake appeared below, and a moment later the sprawling prefabricated buildings of the camp, enclosed within an electrified metal-mesh fence. Dall dropped the flitterjet toward the ground, but didn't try to land at once; certain formalities had first to be gone through, lest a carefully camouflaged anti-aircraft gun send a hail of shells streaking up at him.

Putting the ship into a low circle over the camp, he switched on the tiny two-way radio built into the control panel, tuning to a special band. A voice spoke almost at once, tense, demanding.

"Who is it?"

"Dall; Harvey Dall."

"Says you, mister. Give the word."

"Ozone."

"Okay. Come on down, Mr. Dall."

There was a tiny landing field at the west end of the enclosure, with a hanger at one side, through the opened doors of which a number of parked craft were visible. Bringing the flitterjet down to a gentle, almost vertical landing, Dall changed the thrust of the overhead jets and sent the ship taxiing toward the hanger. As he climbed out a mechanic came running up, features widened in a welcoming grin. Dall grinned back, though inwardly he felt a twinge of something that closely approached disgust. He could very well have parked the ship himself, but Frontenac insisted on having servants perform all chores, regardless of how slight they might be.

In another moment Dall shrugged; Frontenac was footing the bills, and it was only fair that he should have his own way.

Besides, there was no denying the fact that Frontenac could well afford his extravagances. He had inherited a fortune on the death of his father, and then, playing the stock market in a manner over which hardened speculators still shuddered or marveled, he had increased the money to several times its original amount. Whether his success was due to blind luck or to extraordinary shrewdness, no one had ever been able exactly to determine; but Dall guessed it was the latter.

JULES FRONTENAC was something of a paradox: at once fiery and impetuous, at once cool and calculating. He was a man of many facets, who threw himself into the pursuit of scientific knowledge with the same vigor with which he plunged after the ball on a polo field, or hurled a strat-rocket through the tenuous upper reaches of the atmosphere in the setting of new speed records. The construction of the *Frontier* was the latest of his many interests. Dall, after the destruction of his own rocket, had been hired as chief engineer and construction superintendent in general. After more than a year of constant, often grueling work—work in which Frontenac himself had enthusiastically and indefatigably taken part—Dall had come to know Frontenac well. Whatever others might think or say about the eccentric, volatile little man, Dall had to admit that he liked him.

These thoughts passed through Dall's mind as he strode from the field, toward the prefabricated cabin that he shared with Frontenac. He was halfway there, when he abruptly became aware of a man crossing to intercept him. The arrival was tall, heavy-set, with bluntly handsome features topped by a close-fitting cap of crisp-curling red hair. He waved a hand at Dall and said:

"I've been looking for you. Nobody seemed to know where you went."

"Just flew up to Chicago for a while, Bruce," Dall returned. "Business, but nothing you would call important. Finish your check-up?"

Bruce Melgard nodded, falling into step with Dall. He was head of the technical staff at the camp, having been there nearly as long as Dall himself. He was nominally under Dall, though there were times when Dall had the disturbing impression that Melgard could at any time have easily taken over and done just as well—if not better. Melgard was pleasant and friendly enough, but there was something vaguely odd about him that Dall could never explain.

"The circuits are all okay," Melgard said. "And the relays function perfectly. The ship is just rarin' to go."

"And she'll go," Dall said, with an undertone of grimness.

Melgard's answering grin held a suggestion of diffidence. "Which reminds me; I haven't given up hope yet. Isn't there some way you could possibly squeeze me in on the flight?"

Dall shook his head. "No room, Bruce. The ship, as you know, can only accommodate two; and with the instruments Frontenac insists on lugging along, it'll be a close fit even at that."

Melgard sighed. "I don't give up easy—but I guess this is it."

"Keep hoping," Dall advised. "If Frontenac and I return in one piece, there'll be other flights." The cabin had been reached; Dall nodded to Melgard and strode toward the door.

Frontenac was seated at a table in the small but luxuriously furnished living room, tinkering with a very large, and obviously very expensive, camera. His thin, dark features broke into an instant smile at sight of Dall, and he bounced to his feet in one of the swiftly impulsive motions characteristic of him. Words burst from his lips in a rush.

"Ah—it's Harvey! I thought I heard a ship land. That box—the injectors, eh? Did you have any trouble on the trip?"

"No trouble," Dall said. He deposited his burden on the table, dropped his hat over it, and settled in a deep chair nearby. He watched Frontenac as he produced and lighted a cigarette.

FRONTENAC'S sensitive features mirrored conflicting emotions; relief and disappointment showed on it in turn. He was well below average height, slender, with large, heavily-lashed dark brown eyes and thick black hair, disordered by repeated nervous combing with his fingers. High cheekbones, together with a narrow, arching nose and thin, mobile lips, gave his face an intense, rapier-like quality. He wore whipcord breeches and highly polished riding boots. A vividly patterned red scarf was knotted around his throat and tucked into the open collar of his powder-blue gabardine shirt. He said slowly:

"No trouble?"

"Well…not exactly," Dall amended.

"Hah!" Frontenac leveled an accusing finger. "Holding out on me, eh? What happened, Harvey? Come on—give."

Dall drew at his cigarette, hesitating. Merrick hadn't mentioned that Dall was to keep secret his new identity as Special Secret Service Operative, evidently leaving the matter to his own discretion. Where persons could be implicitly trusted, there apparently were no objections to Dall revealing himself; and Dall knew that Frontenac could be trusted.

But Dall didn't explain at once. He glanced at a doorway across the room and asked, "Is Jerome in?" Jerome was Frontenac's valet, secretary, and handy man in general.

Frontenac shook his head with a quick, bird-like motion and dropped into a chair opposite Dall. "Why all the mystery, Harvey? What happened to you anyway?"

Leaning forward, Dall softly related the story of his two encounters with Metz and Bushnell and of his meeting with Merrick and Weston that had resulted. He repeated substantially what Merrick had told him about the rocket disasters and the motive behind them, finishing with the honor that had been conferred upon him in return for his pledge to help.

Frontenac's expression was one of deep awe. "Special Operative—think of it! And you deserve it, Harvey; you already suspected all those things a long time before that man, Merrick, told you about them."

Dall shrugged. "The disasters make a pattern that's pretty easy to see. And it's probable that the Secret Service was interested in them for quite some time before they contacted me. But the fact that the Secret Service is interested does mean I wasn't just doing a lot of high-powered guesswork. We now have all the more reason for wanting to reach the Moon safely. And we must be more than ever careful to see that nothing happens to the *Frontier.*"

"Not to mention ourselves," Frontenac said. A bleak shadow touched his face. "But only until we complete our mission successfully. After that, our lives—as before—mean nothing." A swift grin removed the shadow from his face; he leaped from the chair. "A toast, Harvey! We must drink a toast!" He whirled and hurried from the room, returning moments later with a bottle and two glasses. Filling them, he handed one to Dall and raised the other high. "To Special Operative Harvey Dall—and the solution of the mystery on the Moon!"

Dall grinned, touched his glass to Frontenac's, and drank. He said slowly, "Something else happened today, Jules."

FRONTENAC'S dark features jerked in astonishment. "Something else? But, good Lord, Harvey, after what you've told me, how could anything else possibly have happened?"

"Remember me telling you about that white-haired man I met while taking a walk a couple of weeks ago? Well, I saw him again, today. At the Loop terminal. He saw me, too. I'm sure he knew I was going to be there."

Frontenac was silent, staring.

"At first," Dall went on, "I thought he was connected with Metz and Bushnell, but it turned out that he wasn't. Who is he connected with, then? With *They*—the organization that's blocking rocket research? If he is, it means that the Secret Service isn't the only group that has a direct line into camp; it means that *They* also have someone checking on us."

"A spy in camp," Frontenac breathed. "An enemy under our very noses…"

Dall nodded somberly. "The *Frontier* is already being carefully guarded, but it might be a good idea if we followed a policy of watching the watchers. At least for the next two nights. It's certain that any attempt to destroy the ship will be made at night, when only the guards are around. And since they're only human, we can't take the risk that one of them might fall asleep on the job and give someone a chance to slip into the hangar."

Frontenac protruded a lean chest and jabbed it with a forefinger. "Then, Harvey, I insist on taking the first watch. Action is what I want—action! I'm tired of all the checking, planning, and figuring that we've had to do. I'll watch tonight. And if I catch anyone sneaking around"—he shook a fist, dark eyes flashing—"I'll blow him to kingdom come!"

The arrangement suited Dall; it gave him the last watch, which he considered most important. It was quite possible that an attempt to destroy the *Frontier* would be made on the very last night before the time set for its take-off. He spoke a few words of agreement to Frontenac and glanced at the plain platinum watch strapped to his wrist that had replaced the more ornate gold one that he had worn previously. Almost time for supper, he saw. He would have to hurry if he wanted to wash and change from his suit into more comfortable clothes…

LONG shadows of evening were stretching over the camp, when Dall and Frontenac left the mess cabin. Most of the little group of mechanics and technicians still at the camp had already preceded them, strolling toward the bunkhouse, where they would play cards or watch and listen to the 'vision set until the time came to turn in. These would remain until the *Frontier* finally left on its trial flight, in case any last-minute repairs or adjustments were necessary.

In unspoken agreement, Dall and Frontenac directed their steps toward the construction hangar, which was situated at one end of the camp's tiny airfield. Four armed guards were on duty outside the hangar, placed at strategic points, and two more were stationed inside. The guards consisted of two groups, working in six-hour shifts. They had been chosen with all possible care, and in addition they were divided into teams of two men, each of whom had strict orders to watch constantly both the other and the men of other teams. The pairings were rearranged each day, so that there would be no slackening of alertness due to familiarity. The mechanics and technicians functioned in a like manner; no one man or team ever did anything in or around the ship that was not watched by another man or team.

It was Dall who had imposed this precautionary system, and the men, fully aware of the stark necessity behind it, co-operated whole-heartedly. There had thus far been no attempts at sabotage, but Dall knew that the real test was yet to come. The unknown spy and potential saboteur whom it was certain the camp harbored may not have been frustrated at all, but only waiting for a certain time or set of circumstances in which to strike. He was backed by a cunning and powerful organization whose record of past successes indicated it would not give up easily.

The guards at the hangar admitted Dall and Frontenac without challenge. Other persons, however, would not have been passed as readily; permission from Dall or Frontenac, even on work projects, was required first. The present group of guards had just come on duty, having finished their meal in the mess cabin a short time after Dall and Frontenac arrived there. Then the group relieved had appeared for their meal.

The hangar lights had been turned on in anticipation of darkness. Under the fluorescents the *Frontier* was a huge, silvery shape, its tapering nose pointed toward the hangar doors. The two guards stationed inside were posted one at each end of the ship. They nodded at Dall and Frontenac, but the two had eyes only for the *Frontier*.

TO THOSE who possessed an artistic rather than a technical sense, the *Frontier* would have seemed a curiously ungainly craft. It completely lacked the cigar-shaped symmetry that one more or less unconsciously expected of a vessel built to navigate the void between worlds. From a slim, pointed bow it widened to a broad, flaring stern, a design that gave the ship a disproportionate, rear-heavy appearance.

To a rocket engineer, however, the *Frontier* would have seemed a marvel of compactness, utility, and strength. That clumsy-looking stern would have been seen at once as the only means of locating the huge jets tubes with a minimum of space and a maximum of mechanical efficiency. And when the difficulties of taking off and landing in a gravitational pull were considered, certain other advantages of its design became apparent: in taking off, it would have a high angle of trajectory, which would conserve fuel; in landing—accomplished stern foremost—it would have greater stability, reducing the danger of its losing balance and crashing when settling down on its jets.

The *Frontier's* flaring stern was channeled to form four great thick vanes or fins. Seen from the rear, these made a cruciform outline, with a large exhaust tube in the center and four smaller ones at the tip of each arm. The smaller tubes slanted outward, so that their jet streams would emerge at an angle relative to the stream from the central tube, thus making it possible while in flight to steer the ship in any desired direction.

The *Frontier* was approximately sixty feet long. Less than a third of this was passenger space; the rest was almost completely taken up by fuel tanks and propulsion engines. The hull was of a smoothly welded, highly-polished beryllo-steel alloy, tough enough to deflect small, low velocity meteorites, though Dall knew it would be no proof against large ones traveling at high speed. Only an impossible thick hull would resist penetration by the latter. Dall was trusting in sheer, blind luck to avoid them, but he had made certain arrangements in case of an emergency.

Thick, blunt wings projected from the vessel's sides, near the bow. These were telescoped at present, but could be extended for use in the atmosphere. Amidship, at the top, was a transparent quartzite pilot shell. Quartzite was the latest product of scientific ingenuity; enormously strong, it at once permitted clear visibility and acted as a shield against both harmful space radiations and the burning ultra-violet rays of the sun.

Dall and Frontenac gazed in silent worship at their creation. To them the *Frontier* had everything of artistic beauty and something over and above mere engineering perfection: it embodied in material things the dream of reaching the far-off stars, which man has always dreamed; in it was crystallized more than a year of work, worry, and hope.

Looking at the ship, Dall felt an abrupt surge of anger that anyone should wish to destroy something so fine. For more than the efforts and ambitions of two men were threatened— the very aspirations of the human race itself were at stake: the race that had labored through countless generations over evolution's long road, reaching out for the stars, until it stood finally on the threshold of fulfillment. And that threshold was here, Dall realized; here, in this very room; here, before him. Beyond it were new worlds, new knowledge, a new and finer life. Nothing, he told himself grimly, must take away the chance to achieve those things.

At last Dall turned and glanced questioningly at Frontenac. The other nodded.

"I'm staying, Harvey. Turn in and get some rest. And"— Frontenac produced a large automatic from under his leather jacket—"don't worry. Everything will be all right."

Dall grinned, waved, and strode from the hangar. Undressing for bed in the cabin, he yawned deeply. He seemed more tired than he realized. Then it struck him as odd; he had done nothing strenuous or exhausting that day.

THE sense of strangeness persisted. He stretched out under the covers, feeling a dull lassitude creep over him. And then he noticed something wrong with his eyes; he seemed unable to focus them properly. The shadowed outlines of the room persisted in blurring, melting together. Even the pattern of his thoughts grew hazy, as though a dark fog was filling his mind, obscuring them.

Something was wrong, he realized dimly. These sensations weren't the sort he normally experienced when tired, even when very tired, which he knew he had no reason to be right now.

The answer burst upon him abruptly. Drugged! He had been drugged; it was the only explanation.

Horror flaming through him, he whipped the covers aside and struggled from the bed. He was breathing heavily. A cold perspiration beaded his face. He swayed dizzily; the outlines of the room whirled before him. Strength was oozing from him; it took terrific effort to remain erect.

Drugged! But how had it happened? Except for supper he had taken nothing internally that might account for his present state.

Supper. *Supper!* Of course. That was the answer. His food had been doped.

And then an even greater horror overwhelmed the first surge he had felt.

Had just his food been doped? Or was it possible that *all* the food had been treated? He realized, even as consciousness flickered like a flame in a rising wind, that little would have been accomplished by drugging him alone. If the use of narcotics indicated an attack on the ship, it would be only logical to remove all potential interference. And everyone at camp had eaten supper—Frontenac, the hangar guards...

The hangar—he had to reach the hangar! Within seconds the ship would be entirely unguarded, wide open to attack.

Moving through sheer force of will rather than strength, Dall lurched toward the door. He seemed to be wading through a thick, transparent jelly. The world spun crazily; a confused roaring filled him; the dark fog in his mind grew darker, spread.

Somehow he reached the door, fumbled it open. A cool breath of evening wind touched his feverish, wet face. It was the last thing of which he was aware, for suddenly he was falling—falling into an endless, utterly black and starless void...

CHAPTER FOUR

AWARENESS was a long, torturous uphill road, and Dall was climbing it slowly, painfully. Something seemed to urge him on; something that he seemed to sense rather than hear.

Up...ever up...

Dall opened his eyes. The cool wind was still there, and the light hadn't yet gone out of the sky. He felt a dull surprise; he couldn't have been unconscious for more than several minutes. How had he come to awaken so soon?

He became conscious of someone kneeling at his side. He squinted, trying to see, through the dusk and the mist still clouding his vision, who it was. He gasped, staring in amazed disbelief.

It was the white-haired man.

The stranger returned Dall's stunned gaze calmly. Nothing moved behind the steady regard of his intense, dark all-knowing eyes. The expression on his pale, smooth face was one of aloof serenity.

Then Dall noticed that the stranger's hands were moving busily over some task. With a wad of some white stuff that seemed to be cotton, he was wiping the needle of a glittering hypodermic syringe. As Dall watched in dazed wonder, the other produced a small case from his coat; the hypodermic was carefully placed within it; and then the case and the wad of cotton vanished into a pocket.

Dall suddenly found words. "*You,*" he whispered. "You're the one who did it—the one who drugged the food. You're after the ship. You're—" Dall started erect, harsh lines leaping into the corners of his mouth and eyes.

Quite suddenly, he was unable to move. He was rigid, frozen in the act of rising. The white-haired man had reached out no detaining hands; nor had he spoken or changed position in the slightest. But abruptly Dall was unable to move.

Something stirred in Dall's mind: a voice that was not a voice, speaking words without sound.

"You do not understand."

The stranger's lips hadn't moved; nothing audible had issued from him; but Dall knew he had spoken. Awe and startled wonder rushed through Dall—like a cold wind. There was only one explanation for the words he had understood, but hadn't heard—telepathy. Somehow, through some inexplicable ability, this white-haired mystery-man possessed the ability to communicate telepathically with others.

Dall's surprise was forced back by stronger emotions. "I'm sure that I do understand," he said grimly, using his voice even though certain, from what had happened a moment before, that it wasn't necessary. "You're planning to destroy the ship. Why else would you be here right now? Why else should you have been sneaking around the camp two weeks ago—and followed me to the city this afternoon?"

"It is as I have said," the stranger returned in his uncannily silent way. "You do not understand. I do not plan to destroy your space vessel; on the contrary, I have come here to prevent it from being destroyed. That is why I have revived you."

Dall's thoughts whirled in bewildered confusion. "A trick," he breathed at last. "It has to be a trick."

"I assure you it is no trick. If it was my intention to destroy your space vessel, it would have been foolish to revive you and thus invite interference."

"Then what are you doing here?" Dall demanded.

"There is no time to explain. Both you and your space vessel are in danger. You must overcome this danger through your own efforts." The stranger paused momentarily, looking in the direction of the hangar, seeing something Dall couldn't see. Then he turned back to Dall, and for the first time expression touched his face—a sudden flash of tension. "You must hurry. Too much time has already been wasted."

HE ROSE, then a smooth, liquid movement that seemed without effort. He turned, walked around the near corner of the cabin, and was gone. Bare seconds later, Dall hurried after him, impelled at once by curiosity and the urgent demands of unanswered questions. And as on that day in the forest, two weeks before, he found nothing.

Dall shrugged aside his annoyed disappointment; more important matters required his attention just now. He peered through the deepening gloom, at the hangar, the white-haired stranger's warning suddenly sharp in his mind. The lights were still on; he could see them shining behind those of the hangar windows visible to him from his position near the cabin. Nothing moved. The camp was very still. A deep hush layover it that was unnatural, ominous.

Everyone else in camp seemed under the effects of the drugged food. But if the stranger was to be credited, someone—or something—was in the hangar. Something that threatened danger to Dall and the *Frontier*. Who—or *what?* Dall intended to find out.

He whirled and hurried into the cabin. He took his automatic from under the pillow where he had placed it in preparing for bed. He was in pajamas, barefooted, but there was no time to dress. Returning outside, he set out at a swift trot toward the hangar.

He had progressed as far as the next cabin, when abrupt sound broke the stillness. There was the faint noise of a door opening and closing, followed by the rapid thuds of approaching feet. Someone was coming from the direction of the hangar— evidently from the hangar itself.

Senses leaping, Dall darted around the side of the cabin near which he had halted. He crouched in tense waiting, his entire consciousness focused upon the advancing footsteps.

A man hurried into sight in the space between the cabin against which Dall was hiding and the one, several yards away, from which Dall had emerged scant minutes before. It was still light enough for Dall to make out details of the other's appearance. Shocked recognition flared into his eyes.

Melgard! Bruce Melgard, the head technician.

There was a gun in Melgard's hand. And even in the dusk, there was that about his figure which seemed grim, menacingly purposeful.

Dall watched in perplexity. Had Melgard also been revived by the white-haired stranger? Or had he been awake all along, having been connected somehow with the drugging of the food?

Within instants came an answer; reaching the cabin that Dall shared with Frontenac, Melgard slowed, crept forward with unmistakable caution. Whoever Melgard thought was in the cabin, he obviously considered an enemy. That person could only be Dall himself. And if Melgard knew or suspected that the white-haired man was somewhere about, his actions could only mean that he considered the stranger an enemy, too.

It was clear, then: Melgard had been responsible for the drugging of the food; Melgard was a member of the organization Dall knew only as *They*.

A bleak purpose formed within Dall. He had to capture Melgard. The man undoubtedly possessed vitally important information regarding *They*. But even more important just now, he had to be stopped in whatever he was up to.

Melgard was moving slowly toward the open doorway of the cabin. The angle of the building shortly hid him from sight, but Dall knew he must now be preparing to enter. Crossing swiftly and noiselessly the space between the two cabins, Dall sidled with infinite care toward the door, taking up a position to one side. Melgard would soon find the cabin unoccupied. And when he emerged—

BUT already the other was moving toward the doorway; moving fast, as though in consternation and alarm. He burst outside; Dall leaped at his back.

Melgard should have gone down under the surprise and force of Dall's onslaught. What actually did happen was something for which Dall was entirely unprepared.

With bewildering, incredible speed, Melgard bent almost double, heaving powerfully to one side. Dall went flying over his shoulders to land with stunning impact on the ground. Dazed, Dall lay there, striving for full understanding of what had happened. A chilling thought struck him: What sort of a person was Melgard anyway? His reactions evidently weren't those of an ordinary man; he'd had only the merest instant's warning of Dall's attack, yet that had been enough.

Melgard stood watching Dall, a slight smile on his blunt features. His gun was pointed with alert steadiness. He had managed somehow to retain his grip on the weapon— something Dall had failed to do with his own, which he had lost in his fall.

Melgard abruptly released a curt, dry laugh and said, "You were a fool to think you could take me, Dall."

"If you'll put that gun away," Dall returned evenly, "I'll see if I can't convince you otherwise."

Melgard shook his head. "Sorry, I haven't any time to waste. You're going with me to the hangar, and then you, Frontenac, and I are going to take a little trip. A one-way trip."

"To the Moon?" Dall asked.

Melgard said slowly, "It could be the Moon."

"You're the one responsible for the drugged food served at supper, aren't you?" Dall asked again.

Melgard nodded. "How does it happen that you're the only one who didn't go under?"

"A little trick I have. Tell me something else. Just who are you working for?"

"The Phrenarch of Lunapolis," Melgard answered unhesitatingly. He laughed in grim amusement at Dall's blank stare. In another moment his face hardened; he gestured with the gun. "Enough of this. The effects of the drug will be wearing off shortly, and I want to be gone before the others start coming around. Come on, Dall, get up."

Dall had been sitting on the ground. He turned over slowly now, started to push himself erect. For an instant he was crouched, poised on fingertips and toes like a dash runner awaiting the signal. He'd already experienced Melgard's uncanny swiftness, and he doubted that he could accomplish what was in his mind, but he didn't hesitate as he threw himself at Melgard's legs, directly under the threatening muzzle of Melgard's gun.

The gun went off—not once, but several times, all in the space of a single heartbeat. The reports of each shot shattered the unnatural stillness of the camp as repeated hammer blows shatter glass. And then Dall hit Melgard, and together they went toppling backward to the ground. But Melgard was in motion even as he fell; with flashing speed, he brought down the barrel of the gun, clubbing it at Dall's head.

THEY hit the ground. Dall landed half atop Melgard, pain bursting and tearing within him from the blows on his head. His consciousness flickered dangerously on the verge of extinction, but with that strange heightening of senses under stress, he was vividly aware of the danger; it underscored as though in searing flame the terrible fire-bright, chilled-steel desperation already inside him. And something happened.

A man is blind; for most or all of his life, he has been without sight. One day he falls, and in the pain, the shock, and the fright of it, he regains his vision.

A man is helplessly paralyzed; has been for most or all of his life. And one day he is subjected to an emotional stress so great, so mind-wrenchingly violent, that he regains the use of his muscles.

Something like that happened to Dall. His mind suddenly clear, with a strange new clarity; his body was filled with a new, vibrant leaping strength. The scene, and all the colors, details, and meanings of it, were suddenly sharp and vivid, like a stereo-photo caught in perfect focus.

Melgard's body had hardly touched the ground, when again he was moving with the amazing swiftness characteristic of him. An ordinary man would have been briefly stunned by the fall, but already Melgard was in furious, deadly action. He no longer tried to use his gun as a club. Twisting under Dall, he whirled himself half erect, whipped up the weapon—aimed it, his finger tightening simultaneously on the trigger. His first shots had missed Dall. It didn't seem possible that he could miss again.

With the curious feeling of strength and clarity of perception that had come to him, Dall missed nothing of Melgard's maneuver. And even as Melgard raised the gun, even as Melgard's finger squeezed the trigger, Dall, too, was moving.

The gun roared—but the bullet failed to reach its target. The breath of an instant before the shot, Dall's hand had flashed forward, knocking up and to one side the barrel of Melgard's weapon. Now Dall's hand closed over the gun; with a burst of savage strength, he twisted it back and down, forcing it violently from Melgard's grip. The gun came free, but before Dall could take advantage of its possession, Melgard exploded into frantic effort. Seizing Dall's arm—the only immediately strategic portion of Dall's body available to him at the moment—he jerked viciously to one side, lunging in the same direction in an attempt to pin Dall beneath him. Dall, however, threw himself quickly in the line of pull, and with the combined motions of Dall's body and his own, Melgard rolled completely over Dall.

Melgard seemed to go wild. He had retained his grip on Dall's gun arm, and his fingers were like gouging bands of steel as he sought furiously to regain the weapon. He writhed and heaved in a frenzy of straining muscles, fighting for a position that would give him the necessary leverage. Grimly, with an icy determination that withstood the consuming heat of battle, Dall countered each raging attack as it came. One thing was vividly clear to him; he must not lose the gun.

Back and forth over the ground the two men struggled, rolling and twisting in a volcanic welter of whipping bodies and threshing legs. Melgard was slowly weakening Dall's grip, but he was using both hands to do it. Dall had one hand free. Again and again he evaded some potentially bone-snapping hold, and then he awoke to the advantage he had in his free hand. He abruptly shifted from the defensive, and began driving in blow after smashing blow to Melgard's chest and middle.

FORCED to protect himself, Melgard released one hand from Dall's gun arm. Dall had been hoping for that. With a tremendous heave, he threw himself off Melgard, and then, knees braced against the ground, he wrenched and jerked at his imprisoned arm—and Melgard's clutch broke. Instantly Dall scrambled completely erect, swaying, breathing in harsh gasps. Melgard followed; and as he started to his feet, Dall suddenly rushed. His fist was sweeping up as he moved, following an arc that started near his knees, drove through Melgard's tardily upflung arms, and landed with a sharp thud against Melgard's jaw.

All the tired savagery went out of Melgard's face. He staggered backward a few steps, eyes glazing. Then he collapsed disjointedly to the ground. He didn't move again.

The deep quiet held once more. Dall stood rubbing his bruised knuckles, a grave satisfaction filling him. The *Frontier* was safe now—not to mention Frontenac and himself. And with Melgard a prisoner, many things would be explained. Light would be shed at last on the identity and motive of *They*. It would no longer be necessary to grope blindly in the dark.

Melgard would talk, Dall assured himself grimly. A man could always be made to talk. And in the present instance, too much was at stake to be squeamish about the means used to make him do so.

Through the silence, the sound of approaching footsteps abruptly became audible; slow footsteps, advancing with unmistakable caution. A voice called softly:

"Bruce? Bruce, is that you? What happened?"

Dall's mind flared in discovery. A confederate! Melgard had a confederate!

Dall didn't move. The newcomer would be armed, and he already sensed that something was wrong. Tensely statuesque, Dall waited, eyes straining at the dusk. The butt of Melgard's gun was hard and cold in his hand.

CHAPTER FIVE

SLOW seconds dragged past. In a far corner of Dall's mind quick thoughts moved.

Melgard's partner, he decided, must have been waiting in the hangar while Melgard left to fetch Dall, supposedly unconscious from the effects of the drugged food. Melgard's shots had alerted the man, but the fight, swift and short, had been over before he had time to arrive on the scene. It was likely that he had not rushed out even then, but had approached slowly, on guard against danger.

Watching intently, Dall presently discerned in the dusk the darker outline of a man. The other was hugging the wall of the opposite cabin, moving forward with extreme slowness.

"Bruce?" he called again. "What's the matter?"

"Drop your gun!" Dall snapped. "I have you covered."

His answer was a sudden roar of shots. But it was an answer he had expected. He had dropped silently to the ground even as he spoke the last word. And now, elbows propped firmly, he took painstaking aim—squeezed the trigger once. The gun crashed, jerking in his fist.

There was a choked cry. Utter silence followed the sound, flowing around and over it like a thick liquid. And then, through the silence, came the sodden thud of a body hitting the ground.

Dall waited, suspecting a trick. But as the leaden minute crept by, no sound or motion came from the other. Dall grew aware of a pebble under him, pressing against his chest. He worked it out slowly, without relaxing his vigil. Then he flipped it a short distance to one side. The noise made by the pebble as it hit the ground was loud in the stillness. Nothing happened; there was no responding barrage of gunshots.

At last Dall rose cautiously to his feet, prepared at any instant to leap aside. Again nothing happened. After a moment, he walked slowly toward the dark shape huddled on the ground in front of the cabin opposite the one near which Dall and Melgard had fought, and from near which Dall had fired.

Melgard's confederate, he found, was dead. Firing at the dim, pale blur of the man's face, Dall had managed to hit him also directly between the eyes, just above the bridge of the nose.

A feeling of sickness lurched giddily through Dall at the realization that he had taken a life. He knew that the man had meant to kill him; that he had undoubtedly taken other lives in the past; and that if he had lived he would certainly take more lives in the future. But the knowledge provided Dall with little comfort. Good or bad, a life is still a life.

Moreover Dall had known the dead man. He had been one of two cooks employed at the mess cabin. How Melgard had managed to put a drug into the food was now clear. He had accomplished it through the aid of a partner, the entire coup obviously having been planned long in advance. The precautionary two-man team system hadn't included the cooks, and it evidently had been a simple matter for Melgard's confederate to drug the food without notice.

DALL returned to where he had left Melgard. Gripping the other under the shoulders, Dall dragged him into the cabin nearby. There was no time to look for rope; Dall secured instead a generous handful of Frontenac's expensive nylon ties. The material was strong, and would serve just as well in a pinch.

Dall bound Melgard carefully. Then, as his pajamas hung in tatters; he hurried into the clothes he had laid aside in preparing for bed. These tasks over with, he set out at a run for the hangar.

The four guards who had been on duty outside the building lay in the positions in which they had fallen. They had not been harmed. Nor, Dall discovered shortly, had the two guards inside been touched. But Frontenac was nowhere in sight.

A cold dread momentarily touched Dall. Then he noticed that the entrance hatch of the *Frontier* was open, and that the lights within the ship had been turned on. Gun gripped at the ready, he entered. He found Frontenac, trussed securely, in the small low cabin situated just under the control room. No one else was present; Melgard and the cook obviously had been the only immediate enemies.

Carrying Frontenac from the ship, Dall set to work unfastening his bonds. He was almost through, when the other stirred and muttered unintelligibly. Dall recalled Melgard's remark about the effects of the drug wearing off soon. Evidently the deadline had now been reached.

But it might be long minutes yet before Frontenac was fully conscious, and Dall didn't intend to be idle that long. Melgard would be recovering from Dall's knockout punch about this time also. Despite the fact that Melgard had been thoroughly tied up, Dall thought it best to keep the man under close watch. Nothing concerning Melgard could be taken for granted; his abilities were beyond the ordinary.

Hurrying to a washroom at one corner of the hangar, Dall soaked a towel in cold water. He bathed Frontenac's wrists and temples, alternating with periods of slapping and massage.

Presently Frontenac's eyelids began to flutter. And then he opened his eyes. He stared, blinking, as though trying to bring Dall's face into focus. After a moment he smiled; evidently he was able to use his eyes now, and had recognized Dall.

"Went to sleep," he murmured in explanation. "Got tired— so tired." Abruptly he sat up, eyes flaring wide. "Harvey!

Something's wrong. I didn't want to go to sleep—I had to. Harvey—*I think I was doped.*"

Dall nodded quickly. "You were and the same thing happened to everyone else at camp, including me."

Frontenac gasped. "But how did it happen?"

Tersely, in staccato sentences, Dall explained. He told of how Melgard had drugged the food served at supper, through the aid of a confederate who had been working as a cook in the mess cabin. He sketched Melgard's motive: the destruction of the *Frontier,* and simultaneously the kidnapping of Frontenac and Dall. Hastily describing how he had been revived by the mysterious white-haired stranger, Dall related his fight with and capture of Melgard, and his killing of Melgard's confederate.

FRONTENAC squeezed his eyes shut and shook his head. "What a world—what a life!" Then he flashed one of his swift grins. "But I like it. And to think of all the fun I missed! I wanted action—and then slept all the way through it…"

"I'd better get back to where I left Melgard," Dall said. "He should be awake now, and will bear plenty of watching." He turned sharply as a movement caught his eye; the guard laying near the bow of the *Frontier* was sitting up. Glancing at the other, near the stern, Dall saw the man brush dazedly at his face in evidence that he, too, was coming around.

"It might be a good idea if you remained here for a while," Dall told Frontenac. "You can explain what happened when the others start asking questions. And see that the guard over the ship is resumed."

Frontenac nodded, and Dall hurried away. As he ran toward the cabin in which he had left Melgard, Dall saw that men were beginning to straggle out from the doorways of the other buildings, further back. It was dark now, but in the light streaming from windows and opened doors, Dall was able to notice the fact that the men were all bewildered and confused. He frowned anxiously; the camp was completely disorganized, its defense system utterly out of gear. If anything were to happen before things were once more coordinated, the results would be disastrous.

Reaching the cabin, Dall found that disaster had already struck—Melgard was gone. One of the windows in the room where he had been was broken. The neckties with which he had been bound had almost all been sliced to pieces. Dall realized what had happened: Melgard, recovering, had inched along the floor, to the window. Then he had pushed himself erect by bracing his body against the wall and shoving against the floor with his bound legs. And finally, breaking in the window, he had used the sharp edge of one of the glass shards remaining in the sash to saw loose the cords at his wrists. With his hands free, cutting away the bonds at his feet with another glass fragment had been a simple matter.

An abrupt sound shocked Dall out of his numbed dejection. It was the dull roar of a flitterjet, starting up.

Melgard! The realization burst like a signal flare in Dall's mind. Escaping from the cabin, Melgard had taken advantage of the camp's disorganization to steal one of the flitterjets parked in the aircraft hanger. And now he had more than an excellent chance to make a complete getaway. Dall knew that the men operating the antiaircraft cannon and searchlights—even if they had awakened—would still be too dazed to attempt bringing Melgard down. Dall was all too painfully aware that he could not operate the gun and searchlights alone; and by the time he had obtained the necessary help, it would be too late.

Despair tore at Dall. It was not so much losing Melgard that he found unbearable, as losing the vital information regarding *They,* which Melgard undoubtedly possessed. Deprived of that knowledge, Dall would once more be fighting blindly, in the dark.

Leaping back outside, Dall squinted into the darkness above the airfield. In a moment he found the circle of pale blue light made by the whirling overhead jets of the fugitive ship. He saw the ship itself, lightless, a darker shadow against the night. It was already some fifty feet above ground, and was rising swiftly.

A plan flashed to Dall. If he could not stop Melgard, he could at least follow him in another flitterjet. And as long as the fuel held out, follow him Dall would!

DALL whirled into motion, racing toward the aircraft hanger. As he crossed the airfield, a figure came running from the direction of the construction hanger to intercept him. The automatically operated sliding doors of the construction hanger had been flung open, and in the light from within that streamed through them, Dall saw that the approaching man was Frontenac.

"Harvey!" the other called. "What's the matter? Who was it that just took off?"

"Melgard!" Dall snapped, without pausing. "And I'm going after him!" He continued his plunge toward the aircraft hanger.

The doors were open, but the lights within the broad, squat structure had not been turned on. Dall fumbled for a wall switch, and the overhead fluorescents glowed. The mechanic who was supposed to have been on duty within the hanger lay sprawled out on the floor. A bruise on his jaw showed it was a fist rather than drugs that was responsible for his unconscious state.

Dall found that it was his own personal flitterjet that Melgard had taken. But Frontenac's sleek sportster was an even speedier craft. This, along with a larger, sturdier ship used to ferry in supplies, had not been damaged; Melgard had apparently been in too much of a hurry to bother.

Clambering into Frontenac's ship, Dall suddenly discovered that he wasn't alone. Frontenac himself came crowding into the cabin after him.

"Thought—you'd—leave me—out, eh?" Frontenac panted. "Well—you've got another guess—coming!"

There was not time to argue. Hands darting over the controls, Dall taxied the flitterjet from the hanger and out onto the field. Within another few seconds he had the craft in the air. As he circled the camp, trying to find some trace of Melgard, there was an abrupt, sharp concussion and something screamed past the ship. And almost immediately afterward, the brilliant beams of two large searchlights flashed blindingly into the surrounding darkness.

The members of the camp's antiaircraft unit had belatedly recovered the full use of their respective senses. And to make up for the first ship, which they had allowed to get away, they were swinging into furious action.

With a snarl of rage and disgust, Dall switched on the radio.

"Who is it?" a voice was demanding. "Give the word!"

"Ozone, you boneheads!" Dall yelled. "Ozone! Now shut up and turn off those lights, or I'll—" Briefly and pungently, Dall explained what he would do.

Frontenac, recovered from his first shock, grinned. "I didn't know anything like that could be done to a man, Harvey. Offhand, I'd say it was physically impossible."

"I could hardly be blamed for trying," Dall growled.

The searchlights went out. Dall squeezed his eyes tight shut for several seconds, then once more scanned the night in search of Melgard's ship. He made a second full circuit of the camp, another, and then he caught the tiny red and green moving points of a ship's flying lights far ahead. Melgard seemed to be headed in the direction of the lake that lay near the camp.

FRONTENAC'S sportster was fast, and Dall used all of his not inconsiderable flying skill to coax forth every bit of speed the craft possessed. It tore recklessly through the night; the drone of its jets softening as peak operating efficiency was reached. Dall was bent tensely forward in his pilot seat, peering with dogged persistence into the rushing darkness, at the lights of the fleeing ship ahead.

Slowly the gap between the two ships narrowed. Dall's eyes were fully accustomed to the darkness now, and with the added aid of the illumination from the bright crescent of a half-moon rising in the sky, he was able shortly to make out the shape of Melgard's craft. His lips thinned in a smile of baleful eagerness.

Frontenac's sportster was proving its superiority; Melgard would not escape.

The lake appeared below, silver in the Moon's radiance. Watching, Dall saw Melgard's flitterjet dart suddenly toward the ground. He frowned in perplexity. What was Melgard up to? Was he planning to land and lose himself in the surrounding wilderness? Dall knew that practically nothing would be accomplished by taking such a means to elude pursuit. Melgard would be marooning himself in rugged, primeval country, where people were few and far between. And with the coming of daylight, it would not be too difficult to hunt him from the air.

Melgard was dropping down toward a strip of beach at the far end of the lake. Altering the thrust of the overhead jets, Dall sent his ship hurtling at a slant toward the spot. In another instant he felt Frontenac grip his shoulder.

"Harvey—look!" Frontenac was pointing tensely.

The beach was bright in the moonlit dusk. A short distance beyond it was a black, apparently solid wall of forest. And now, running from the forest and out onto the beach, appeared the figure of a man. As he reached the beach, he stopped, beckoning at Melgard's ship.

Dazed bewilderment swept Dall. The man on the beach seemed to expect Melgard—seemed to know who he was and why he was coming. But how had he known? Almost instantly the answer came to Dall. The radio in Melgard's flitterjet. Melgard had used the radio, tuning to some special wavelength, to contact the other. But where had the man come from? What had he been doing down there, in the forest? Was he alone?

Was he alone?

The thought exploded in Dall's mind. If the man wasn't alone, he and Frontenac were rushing headlong into what might very well be a trap!

Dall sent his hands racing over the controls of the flitterjet. He and Frontenac were jolted sharply backward in their seats as the craft straightened abruptly from its dive. It leveled out, then swept up and around, darting back upon its former course.

Dall flashed a quick look at the beach. Melgard had landed, and now he and the other man were running toward the forest. They were swallowed from sight in the dense black shadows that lay among the close-grouped trees.

"What's the matter, Harvey?" Frontenac queried. "Giving up the chase?"

Dall nodded quickly. "That man we saw down there on the beach may not have been alone. There might be others somewhere in the forest. We can't risk running into a trap. We'll play safe by getting a head start, but if nothing happens we'll circle back to see what they're up to."

Dall turned his attention to flying, while Frontenac watched through the rear windows of the flitterjet's cabin. Abruptly Frontenac emitted a loud gasp.

"You were right, Harvey. Look!"

Whirling in his seat, Dall saw a slim silver shape rising into sight from the black depths of the forest. A ship. And more than that—a space ship! For it had the size and design that only a space ship would have. But it was like no space ship Dall had ever known. It was rising horizontally instead of vertically, the way a space ship should rise. And, incredibly, no rocket exhaust trail showed at its stern; there was nothing at its stern from which a rocket exhaust could emerge. At both ends it tapered smoothly.

Whatever its inexplicable means of propulsion, the mystery ship was moving—moving fast. It rose to the altitude at which Dall held the sportster; and now, still on a horizontal keel, it turned, pointing its slim tapering bow at the flitterjet. Then, with a sudden, effortless soundless rush, it sped forward.

Dall stiffened under the impact of an appalling realization. He burst out:

"Why…why, blast them! They intend to ram us!"

CHAPTER SIX

THE distance between space ship and flitterjet was closing with numbing swiftness. Within mere instants, it seemed, the smaller, lighter craft would be bludgeoned out of the sky—smashed in broken fragments to the ground.

By no stretch of the imagination could space ships as yet be called a common sight. As far as Dall had known, the *Frontier* was the only space-going vessel then in a state of completion. It was thus especially disconcerting to have a full-fledged, perfectly functioning space ship materialize almost literally under his very nose. And the shock was even greater to have that ship hurtle straight at him with unmistakably deadly intent.

Almost too late Dall jerked out of the paralysis brought on by that bizarre, completely unexpected manner of attack. Whirling back to the controls, he sent the sportster into a convulsive leap almost vertically upward. A split second later the strange space ship plunged into the space the flitterjet had occupied.

Keeping the sportster in its climb, Dall saw the space ship sweep around in a great half-circle. Again its tapering bow was pointed in silent menace; again it rushed. This time Dall abruptly cut power and dropped. The deadly silver projectile was thwarted once more, but its pilot evidently had been expecting some such maneuver; for now the half-circle with which it jockeyed back into position was tighter, quicker; and it resumed the attack more slowly, with greater care.

"What a ship," Frontenac marveled huskily. "What a ship. Operating in an atmosphere, in a strong gravitational pull, and yet, what speed—what maneuverability!"

Dall grunted, "If someone pointed a gun at your head, with the intention of blowing your brains out, I suppose you'd still find time to admire the beauty and workmanship of the gun."

Frontenac grimaced wryly; in another moment he sobered, frowning. "There ought to be something we can do to get away…"

"I know we can't keep jumping up and down the way we've been doing," Dall pointed out. "The fuel won't last—even if my nerves do."

The sportster was now moving in a swift arc that was taking it back toward the lake. Dall hoped in this way to prevent the pilot of the space ship from getting a direct aim for another rush. But the other was closing in slowly, apparently with the intention of moving so close that Dall would be unable to evade a sudden lunge.

Dall, however, did not wait for another attack. Over the lake, he put the flitterjet into a swift upward spiral. Again the space ship tried slowly to close in, but now Dall abruptly sent his own craft dropping. Altering the thrust of its jets, he started circling in an opposite direction. Balked in his efforts to creep up on the flitterjet, the space pilot abandoned his crafty stalking tactics. He sent the projectile darting forward, this time not directly at the sportster, but toward the spot where it would be instants later in its circling course.

DALL was almost caught. A sudden burst of speed took him clear of the danger, but with a speed that matched his own the space ship leaped in pursuit. Its pilot evidently had grown impatient, if not actually angry, and now he sent his craft lunging repeatedly at his prey, for all the world like the disembodied head of some venomous snake.

But if the space ship was a snake, Dall's sportster was an agile mongoose, darting, dodging, evading death with hair's-breadth nearness. Time and again, Dall leaped at the last moment to safety; time and again, that deadly silver bullet struck. Dall knew he couldn't keep it up; the intense mental and physical strain of the weird duel was rapidly tiring him. And his eyes, flickering anxiously at the fuel gauge, saw that the indicator needle was hovering dangerously low.

Something had to be done, Dall realized with piercing urgency. Somehow he and Frontenac had to come out of this alive. As Harvey Dall, rocket engineer, his life, except to himself, was comparatively unimportant; but as Harvey Dall, Special Operative of the United States Secret Service, his life mattered a great deal: a great nation, directly, and the world, indirectly, were depending on him for vital information—information regarding a powerful and sinister enemy, with whose representatives he was even now in mortal conflict.

By pure chance rather than design, the sportster was still moving over the lake. Dall abruptly grew conscious of the fact, and as he did so, the light of a plan burst upon him. He and Frontenac might yet have a chance to escape...

Hurriedly, even while his hands flashed over the controls, Dall told Frontenac of his scheme. The smaller man was instantly enthusiastic.

"I think it'll work, Harvey. It *has* to work."

"Everything depends on perfect timing," Dall said. "It's frightfully risky, but we can't keep this up any longer."

Frontenac gripped Dall's shoulder reassuringly. "I'm with you, Harvey—all the way." With that he left his seat beside Dall, removing his safety straps, and went to the door of the sportster's cabin. He crouched there in tense waiting.

Dall bent desperately to work. Deliberately he made the evasive maneuvers of the flitterjet slower, increasingly clumsy, as though he was tiring. And the pilot of the space ship, as the next few seconds showed, was taken in by the trick. With evident eagerness his attacks grew swifter, more reckless.

Then the exact conditions Dall had been waiting for finally arrived. Escaping with apparent awkwardness a particularly furious rush, he secured the time necessary to put the flitterjet into a slow sweeping arc.

He waited tautly for the next attack. This was it, he thought. This was it. Everything depended on what would happen now.

The space ship curved around, crept in, then flashed forward. Dall reacted with frantic haste. The flitterjet dropped with appalling abruptness, almost vertically down, toward the lake. Down…down…

Carried on by its terrific momentum, the space ship grew small with distance. Dall had been hoping for that; those in the projectile would momentarily be unable to observe what the occupants of the flitterjet were doing. And before the murderous spacecraft could swing around and come rushing back, Dall's plan would already be in effect.

THE waters of the lake were leaping up to meet the descending sportster. Dall threw on power to check the fall. And as they slowed, he glanced, nodding sharply, at Frontenac. The other had opened the door of the flitterjet's cabin; now, with an answering nod, he leaped out and down in a dive toward the lake. He hit the water cleanly and disappeared from sight.

Dall started the sportster up again; and as it started, he locked on the automatic pilot, which would hold the ship that way. Then he was scrambling for the cabin door, and a moment later he, too, was plunging down toward the lake.

The water closed over Dall, shocking in its coldness. He seemed to descend endlessly, and then he slowed, became momentarily suspended in the depths, and began to rise. He kicked out with arms and legs, forcing himself to rise slowly.

Breaking surface, he drew quick gulps of air to hungry lungs, peering about him. Frontenac, floating a few yards away, called a soft reassurance. Satisfied that the other was safe, Dall began searching the sky. The crescent Moon was higher now, brighter. It flooded the star-strewn dusk with luminescent, silvery-pale radiance. Soon Dall caught sight of the space ship. The craft was still far off, but it had curved around, and now it was rushing back toward the lake.

"On your toes!" Dall called presently, to Frontenac. "Here she comes!"

The projectile swept in over the lake, hurtling down at the rising flitterjet. It struck its previously evasive target with vengeful force; there was a great tearing crash of sound, sharp and brittle. And then, to all appearances neither staggered nor damaged in the slightest, the projectile rushed on, while the torn and broken fragments of the flitterjet began raining into the lake.

Seconds before the crash, Dall and Frontenac had submerged, each with the firm intention of going down as far as possible—and staying there as long as possible. Luckily enough, none of the larger pieces of the demolished flitterjet struck anywhere near them, while the several feet or so of water between them and the surface acted as a shield against the smaller ones.

The occupants of the space ship were unable immediately to observe the effects of the crash, for the momentum of their shattering charge had carried them irresistibly onward. By the time they returned to the scene, the wreckage of the flitterjet had already sunk from sight. Only ripples, widening over the surface of the lake, remained to tell of what had happened.

The space ship circled slowly a few times. Then, those inside evidently having become certain that their victims had perished, the craft pointed its nose at the sky and began swiftly to rise.

A MOMENT later Frontenac popped from the water, gasping. Dall followed shortly, equally breathless. Together, treading water, they peered upward at the rapidly diminishing shape of the projectile. Higher, it soared, ever higher, growing smaller. And then it was gone, too small any longer to be seen.

"We're safe," Dall told Frontenac. "They think they got us."

"Us?" Frontenac echoed. "But how could they have known we were on the ship?"

"They got close enough a few times to see into the flitterjet's cabin," Dall said. "And it's likely that they didn't depend on moonlight, as we did, but used an infra-red night scanner."

A tremor of growing chill shook Dall; he glanced toward the strip of beach where stood the flitterjet Melgard had abandoned. Not too far away, he noted with satisfaction. Gesturing to Frontenac, he struck out and began to swim.

A quarter of an hour later they were back in camp. Generous doses of brandy, hot baths, and dry clothes threw off the effects of their immersion in the lake. With sleep the most distant thing in their minds just then, they gathered by tacit agreement in the cabin living room.

Frontenac lighted a cigarette, dark brows contracted in a frown. He said slowly, "Melgard may think we're dead, Harvey, but there's still the *Frontier*. He can't be certain that other persons won't try to fly the ship."

Dall nodded gravely. "It's quite probable that he intends to see no one does."

"What do you think he'll do?" Frontenac asked. "With the kind of ship he has, there's the possibility that he may try to approach silently over camp and bomb the *Frontier*."

"I don't think so," Dall said. "That would bring the activities of his organization directly out into the open. Judging by its past actions, this organization will want to stay hidden until ready for whatever it's up to. It's certain that Melgard has orders to destroy the *Frontier*, but it's also certain that those orders are to make it look like an accident. And since he thinks we're out of the way, there's no reason for him to be in a hurry about it. Most likely he intends to wait and see who takes over the ship before stepping in."

Frontenac glanced up from a thoughtful scrutiny of the glowing tip of his cigarette; he smiled thinly. "And he'd do that by planting agents among the persons who hypothetically would take over the ship, eh?"

"Exactly," Dall agreed. "Either among the technicians who would check the ship over before the flight, or among the persons who would take part in the flight itself. Melgard tried this last on us; he practically begged me several times to let him go along on our trial flight. Probably he intended to eliminate us while in space, and then take the ship somewhere where it would never be found again. He tried to follow this plan even after I refused; that was his purpose in drugging the food."

FRONTENAC shook his head for a few seconds in a sort of mild incredulity. "When you stop to think of it, Harvey, all that hocus-pocus and beating around the bush doesn't seem to quite make sense. We've seen the ship that picked Melgard up back there at the lake; we've seen what it can do. All right—why couldn't Melgard simply wait out in space until we—or any others—came along, and then simply riddle us full of holes with a special cannon that wouldn't be hard to build? That way we'd be disposed of quickly and thoroughly, with no risk or evidence."

"Maybe it's because Melgard's ship isn't sufficiently maneuverable in space," Dall suggested. "We already know that its flight principle in no way involves rocket propulsion. How it does move is a mystery; but a good guess would be that it somehow utilizes gravity, or gravitic lines of force. Out in space, then, with the conflicting pulls of earth, moon, and sun acting on the ship, it's probably too difficult to shift quickly from one gravitic field of influence to another, as would be required to pursue a victim and match speed and course, so as to get a cannon to bear. And there's the added difficulty that the victim is almost certain to notice what is going on and do a lot of quick and complicated dodging.

"A further reason," Dall went on, "might be the psychological value of having the attacks take place on Earth instead of in space. On Earth, making the attacks look like accidents, it would appear as though rocket technology was at fault, with the result that rocket research would gradually be discouraged. If rockets left Earth, to be attacked in space, it would prove that there was nothing wrong with rocket technology, while something was radically wrong in space. And since there's nothing men like more than a good mystery, you can bet they'd keep on going to find out just what was wrong in space."

Frontenac had listened quietly, smoking his cigarette. Now, crushing out the stub, he asked with characteristic suddenness, "Harvey, where do you suppose Melgard went in that ship? To the Moon?"

"That's a good possibility," Dall returned. He fingered his jaw, scowling slightly. "But what in the name of reason could be on the Moon? It's airless, dead, certainly uninhabitable, and almost certainly just as uninhabited."

"One side of the Moon is always turned toward Earth," Frontenac reminded. "Who knows what is on the other side—the side we never see? It might be a mistake to judge one by the other."

"You may be right," Dall said. "But it's a sure bet that the two sides of the Moon are almost the same in general appearance and physical properties. It's natural to suppose that the other side might be different—simply because we never see it." He shrugged and fell silent. "And there's the white-haired man," he resumed after a moment. "Who is he? How does he fit in? We know he's friendly; he revived me in time to spoil Melgard's plans. That means he's working against Melgard's organization. But why? What is his motive? Who is behind him?"

Dall rose from his chair and began pacing the floor. Abruptly he swung to Frontenac. "We don't know the answers—but one thing is clear: we have a big advantage right now. Melgard thinks we're dead; he won't be expecting the *Frontier* to leave Earth immediately; he'll be waiting to see who takes over the ship, so he can plan his next moves. And while he's doing that, we'll leave and be on our way to the Moon before he knows or can do anything about it."

A swift grin leaped to Frontenac's expressive lips; his dark eyes sparkled. "We'll get ready at once, Harvey. Why waste time?"

Dall nodded, straightening purposefully. "At once," he agreed.

CHAPTER SEVEN

IT WASN'T so simple in practice; numerous details had first to be attended to before actual preparations for the flight could begin. The personnel of the camp, Dall found, were in a state of alarmed bewilderment. It was still early in the night, and few if any of the men had turned in. Dall, calling them together, was showered with polite yet persistent questions. The men already knew a little of what had happened, but it was necessary for Dall to explain more fully. Swiftly and concisely, he did so.

Even then it was obvious to Dall that many doubts and apprehensions remained. The drugging was hardly an event that the men could dismiss lightly; it was a nerve-shattering climax to the strain under which they had been working for long months. They were demoralized, filled with a sense of insecurity; for despite all precautions against attack, an attack had occurred. And having once experienced the power and cunning of the enemy, they could not be certain that another attack would not occur.

Dall became painfully aware that the men at present were hardly in a state of mind to deal with the delicate and complex details of preparing the *Frontier* for immediate flight. He didn't intend to put things off; it might be dangerous—even catastrophic—to wait. The situation was something he had to whip, and he plunged into it without hesitation.

He explained his purpose in calling the men together, emphasizing the fact that the *Frontier* had to leave at once, and that the task of readying it for the flight demanded the utmost in efficiency and concentration. Almost fiercely he accused the men of their present attitude, pointing out that they had not been harmed in Melgard's attempt, nor were they likely to be harmed a second time. And his inherent leadership qualities made the men respond instinctively to his reassurances; individually and then as a group they indicated their willingness and fitness to start work. At last, certain that he had the men welded into an efficient whole once more, Dall began issuing crisp orders.

As he finished, Dall waved a hand in a gesture of dismissal. It was a peculiar gesture, but the men, turning away to begin their designated tasks, didn't notice—except for one. This man remained behind after the others had gone. Dall recognized the other as a mechanic, a quiet, pleasant-featured youngster. Now, however, Dall knew the man was more than a mere mechanic— he was a Secret Service operative, as his response to Dall's code signal showed. Dall had known there was an operative at camp, but until now he had been unaware of the man's identity.

Dall extended the wrist on which a plain platinum watch was strapped. The youthful operative glanced at it closely; he nodded and said:

"A special, eh? Good work, Mr. Dall." He turned grim. "Anything I can do?"

DALL hadn't forgotten Melgard's dead confederate. He had thought at first of reporting the man's death to the sheriff in a nearby town, but had decided finally to let the Secret Service handle the matter. It was possible that an investigation of the erstwhile cook's background might turn up something that would prove a valuable lead to *They*.

Dall explained this now to the mechanic-operative. He finished, "Another reason why I want the Secret Service to handle this is because the local authorities might somehow allow publicity to leak out. Melgard would be waiting for this; it's vitally important that he doesn't know Frontenac and I are alive until we're well on our way to the Moon."

The operative nodded quickly. "I'll take care of it, Mr. Dall. You can forget this part of the case." Saluting, he hurried out.

Dall followed the others to the construction hanger, where he joined Frontenac in supervising the activities being initiated in and around the *Frontier*. From air conditioning system to rocket motors, the ship was examined carefully, each mechanic or technician working in his own special domain. As reports came in, Dall checked them off on blueprints and charts. It developed that the *Frontier* was as completely in perfect working order as could be determined.

Next Dall had the ship fueled for a ground test and moved outside, to the airfield, where floodlights had already been set up. Hydraulic jacks, special dollies, and a tractor accomplished the quite considerable task of moving the vessel. Dall decided against using a radio remote control hook-up; the process of installing one would have been too time-consuming, and in addition the examination had showed that there was little or no possibility of anything going wrong.

Frontenac insisted on joining Dall in the ship for the test; and when the men outside had cleared away, moving to positions of safety about the edges of the field, Dall started the motors. He kept their action well below lift velocity, and they roared a song of leashed but potent power—a song without sour notes or broken chords, that lasted until the last dregs of fuel had been exhausted.

Grinning one of his rare boyish grins, Dall glanced at Frontenac. "She's all right," he said.

"All right?" Frontenac cried indignantly. "Why, she's perfect. She's superb. She's magnificent! She's—" He choked and gestured wordlessly as though to show how feeble further adjectives were.

The final details were more simple in nature and went swiftly. Fuel was pumped into the ship's tanks, and supplies and equipment loaded aboard. The first traces of dawn had hardly begun to show in the sky, when Dall, who had indefatigably been checking the progress of the work against charts and lists, announced that everything was ready.

Neither Dall nor Frontenac had as yet had any sleep; with the exhilarating knowledge that the *Frontier* stood at last on the brink of its adventure, prepared and poised for imminent flight, neither felt any slightest need for rest. They decided to leave at once.

They donned more appropriate clothing, and over this pulled specially-built, one-piece suits, heavy but flexible, made of a strong, plastic-coated fabric. Airtight, electrically-warmed, and with an independent oxygen supply in tanks fastened to the shoulders, the garments were intended as protection against loss of air, heat, and pressure, as might happen if the ship were struck by meteorites. There were helmets to accompany the suits, which, however, Dall and Frontenac did not put on at once.

Then, making their farewells among the staff, they entered the ship. Dall sealed the entrance hatch, and followed Frontenac up to the control room. They strapped themselves into their huge, thickly rubber-padded spring-cushioned seats, then waited tensely for the signal that would indicate that the field had been completely cleared.

PRESENTLY a flare burst into intolerable brilliance—the signal. No blare of martial music, no thunder of saluting cannon, could have been more eloquent than that simple blaze of light.

Dall poised his hands over the controls. He glanced a moment into the east, where the sun was rising in aureate splendor; his eyes touched the rose-tinted clouds in the brightening sky, went to the shadow-wrapped fields beyond the camp, and looked at last to Frontenac. The other nodded; he understood. This was the Earth—the Earth of clouds and trees, rolling hills and tossing oceans. This was the cradle Man was leaving. Beyond was the Moon…"

Then Dall's face drew into lines of purpose; his hands began moving over the controls with deliberate yet swift precision. A switch turned on the ignition system, and a row of studs connected in all motors. A lever was moved down in its calibrated slot, adjusting the aperture of the injectors for takeoff velocity. Then the fuel lines were opened; fuel sprayed from the injectors was ignited in a continuous, terrific explosion that shot from each individual exhaust tube to merge in a single mighty blast.

The blast paled in color as maximum combustion efficiency was reached; its first thundering bellow dropped in pitch, became a steady, even roar. The *Frontier* began to rise, its bow tipping up; slowly it climbed the flaming ladder of its blast. There was a quality of ponderous, plodding steady deliberation about this initial stage of its take-off that was somehow bizarre. The performance was like nothing so much as a sequence from movie film shown in slow motion. But gradually, and at a rapidly growing rate, the ship's speed of ascent increased, its bow tilting more and more sharply to the vertical. Then it was pointed straight up, streaking faster and ever faster into the rose and gold glory of the dawn.

The mounting acceleration was like a gargantuan hand, pushing with relentless pressure against Dall and Frontenac. It grew ever more difficult to move, though now it was no longer necessary for them to do so; all immediate adjustments had been made, and the ship was already in the first stage of its carefully calculated orbit. They reclined passively in their huge seats, gazes fixed intently upon the dials, gauges, and meters on the instrument board, which told more clearly than their own limited senses could have done the epic story of their flight. Each had donned special goggles to protect his eyes from the increasingly intolerable brilliance of the sun.

The Earth dropped away steadily beneath them; details of the surface dwindled and outlines blurred under the growing depth of atmospheric haze. The acceleration pressure increased. It was impossible to move, almost impossible to breathe. To Dall it was as though an enormous weight pressed upon his body; pain, heavy and dull, beat through him in slow waves. A threatening blackness flickered at the fringes of his mind, growing, closing in.

Time that seemed like centuries crept by—centuries of mercilessly squeezing pressure, tortured breathing, and throbbing pain. The entire continent became visible below them, mist-wrapped, dim and curiously unreal. The western edge of it faded into a blue haze; the eastern edge was brighter, more clearly defined, and beyond it lay the flat, gray-blue expanse of the Atlantic. The sky ahead was a deep indigo, shading slowly to black; stars were visible, already unutterably brilliant and intense. The interior of the *Frontier* was stiflingly hot, filled with the muted roaring of the motors. The ship was still rising vertically; it was not, however, moving in a straight line but along the lower leg of a vast parabola, due to the axial and orbital velocities of the planet from which it has, in effect, been flung.

Gradually the Earth assumed a spherical shape; the acceleration pressure eased away as the ship went beyond the planet's sphere of gravitational influence. No longer was there a sky, only the deep, velvety blackness of airless space, spattered and strewn with countless blazing stars.

THE threatening darkness had almost closed over Dall; now it withdrew, and full awareness returned to him. He was exhausted, his body ached with bruised soreness, but he had a sense of profound relief—the worst of that infernal pressure was gone.

Dall peered at Frontenac. The other was stirring feebly; he blinked several times, as though awakening from a doze. And then, meeting Dall's eyes, he grinned wanly.

Reassured, Dall turned his attention to the instrument board. He studied various dials and gauges, glanced at the chronometer, then compared the readings with data on the chart of the ship's orbit. He made certain corrections of course, cutting the blast from the large central exhaust tube and from two of the four smaller outward slanting fin tubes. He used the two remaining active fin tubes for a carefully timed interval, then turned them off. Only the central tube was brought into play again.

"Nothing to do for quite a while now," Dall told Frontenac. "We'd better get some sleep."

"Sleep," Frontenac snorted in disdain, gesturing at the star-gemmed panorama of space beyond the pilot shell. "And miss all this?"

"You'll be seeing this for some sixty hours more," Dall pointed out. "You won't miss anything. We haven't slept yet, and we'll need plenty of rest for what's ahead."

Frontenac nodded reluctantly. "Guess you're right, Harvey. I am tired, come to think of it."

Dall set the chronometer alarm for six hours ahead; another alarm, connected to the air passage gauges, would sound in the event that penetration of a meteorite caused air to escape from the ship. With no further formalities, he and Frontenac settled themselves in their huge chairs; these were every bit as comfortable for slumber as a bunk or hammock would have been. Within minutes, lulled by the soft roar of the single active motor, they were asleep.

Almost immediately, it seemed, the alarm went off. Dall once more began checking and correcting course, while Frontenac descended to the cabin below, to prepare coffee and sandwiches.

After eating they set up the special camera. It was Frontenac who gave orders now; with one of his characteristically abrupt metamorphoses, he was no longer Frontenac the intrepid explorer, but Frontenac the zealous scientist. Leaving Dall to operate the camera from a convenient porthole, he busied himself with various pieces of scientific equipment, the most immediate of these being a spectroscope, a Geiger counter, and a small telescope.

Thus was their routine established. At frequent intervals, Dall checked and corrected course; every four hours they ate; whenever they felt tired enough to do so—which was not often—they slept; and in between they gathered data with the scientific instruments. They kept busy, and time quickly passed, while the Earth became a great blue-green orb high above them and the Moon swelled into a vast sphere ahead.

AN UNEXPECTED—and entirely unwelcome—break in the monotony of the trip came when they were some fifty hours out. Dall and Frontenac happened to be in the control room at the time, preparing to settle themselves in their seats for a short nap. They were interrupted by the sudden jerking of the ship under the force of an impact. And moments later, while they stared at each other in shocked dismay, there followed the shrill clamor of the air pressure alarm bell.

"We've been hit," Dall gasped. "A meteorite—and a big one, judging from the blow we felt. Get your helmet on…and quick!"

Due to foresight on Dall's part rather than luck, the helmets were in the control room, close at hand. He and Frontenac wore their emergency suits; and it was a matter of mere seconds to snatch up and don the helmets, seal them airtight, and connect the metal hose oxygen intakes to the tanks on their shoulders.

These immediate measures taken, Dall anxiously studied the air pressure gauges for the location of the mishap. He found it was the cabin below the control room that had been struck. The airtight hatch separating the two compartments was already sealed shut, but Dall began testing it, to make certain that no air was leaking from the control room.

The ship jerked again. Dall stiffened, peering tensely about him. As he did so, there was still another shock; hardly ten feet away, at one side of the control room, a jagged hole appeared magically in the wall, and the merest flash of an instant later another showed in the floor. The meteorite had gone through the ship at an angle, piercing its tough metal skin as a hot knife passes through butter.

The air pressure alarm shrilled again. This time air was escaping from the control room.

Dall fought down a surge of incipient panic. No reason to go into a dither; the situation was far from hopeless. The holes in the ship could easily be patched over; spare oxygen tanks in the cabin below would fill the evacuated compartments with a new air supply.

Then Dall's thoughts exploded in abrupt horror. The spare oxygen tanks... If... He began tearing frantically at the clogs fastening down the hatch, which he had been inspecting. Throwing the cover back, he flung himself into the cabin below.

It was as he had feared. One of the meteorites had penetrated at such an angle as to shear through, in a single sweep, the outlet pipes of three entire tanks. One tank had escaped damage solely because a protruding wall girder had forced it to be placed out of line with the others.

One tank left...Dall knew it wasn't enough for Frontenac and him to return to Earth.

CHAPTER EIGHT

DALL looked up slowly as he became aware that Frontenac had followed him to the cabin. The other was staring at the severed outlet pipes; his eyes, behind their helmet lenses, were wide and darkly clouded with appall.

For a long time neither moved. Then Dall straightened, glancing over the compartment walls and floor. Holes in the metal fabric showed in numerous places where the meteorites had pierced in entering and leaving. These could be patched over, but Dall doubted that the effort was worth making at all; with only one remaining tank a sufficient air pressure couldn't be maintained within the ship. A better idea, he decided, would be to save the remaining air supply to replenish the shoulder tanks of his and Frontenac's emergency suits. It would last considerably longer this way—though not long enough to reach Earth.

Frontenac touched Dall's arm, then began to gesture in pantomime. In a moment Dall understood what was wanted of him; he lowered his head to Frontenac's height, so they could touch helmets. Frontenac wanted to say something, but in the near vacuum that now surrounded them, sounds could pass only over some material bridge. Touching helmets accomplished this; words were audible, though curiously metallic in tone and somewhat indistinct.

"Looks like we're sunk, Harvey," Frontenac said. "There won't be enough air to get back on."

"It might not be hopeless," Dall returned.

"What do you mean?"

"There might be something on the Moon—impossible as it seems. People, maybe. The ship in which Melgard tried to ram us was a space ship, you know. And his organization has gone through a lot of trouble to keep others from getting to the Moon."

"But, Harvey, if Melgard's the only one we can depend on for help, it'll be like jumping from the frying pan into the fire. He's already tried twice to get rid of us."

Dall said slowly, "We might be able to find a way out. Anyhow," he added after a moment, "we haven't reached the Moon yet. Maybe—" He gave an abrupt shrug, leaving the sentence unfinished. Straightening, he gestured to Frontenac and pulled himself up the ladder to the control room above.

As he strapped himself into his seat, Dall's eyes, behind their helmet lenses, were as cheerless and forbidding as bits of cold, raw steel. Maybe, he thought darkly, again. Maybe there was nothing on the Moon after all. He and Frontenac might be completely wrong in their theories concerning Melgard. They might actually be the victims of a cunning game of indirection—made to believe something was there that really wasn't.

In that case they were through—irrevocably. They could never hope to return to Earth on the remaining oxygen.

WITH a bleak tightening of his jaw muscles, Dall forced his attention to the controls; the collision with the meteorites had made necessary serious changes in course. When once more the instrument readings corresponded with the data on the flight chart, he sat very quietly, eyes fixed in brooding on the swelling immensity of the Moon. The nap, which earlier he had intended to take, was forgotten; the deadly problem that had arisen, precluded any thought of sleep.

Slow hours dragged by. And then, finally, the instruments showed that the *Frontier* had entered the Moon's gravitational field.

Dall snapped to attention; the next few hours would be critical ones, demanding everything in the way of alertness and piloting skill. First he pressed a stud, which set to spinning a weighted wheel located at the *Frontier's* center of gravity. The panorama beyond the pilot shell gradually shifted as the ship began swinging around; end for end it turned, until the stern instead of the bow was pointed at the Moon. Now the full force of all rockets took up the task of checking the ship's plunge.

The Moon swelled in size, filling all immediate space. In the crescent phase, half of its surface was in brilliant sunlight, the other half in black shadow. Due to the satellite's airlessness, there was no gradual merging of shades; one began, simply and abruptly, where the other left off.

Still the Moon grew, though more and more slowly. The *Frontier's* speed was being checked to the point where it was almost literally floating down on its jets. Then Dall turned off the fin tubes and again started the weighted wheel to spinning. The ship was on the Moon's Earthward side, but now, under Dall's manipulation of the controls, it began moving in an orbit toward the Sunlit hemisphere. Dall was sending it toward the side perpetually hidden from Earth. Few details could be seen as yet; the surface was almost invisible in the blinding white sunlight.

The great blue-green crescent of the Earth seemed to sink in the sky as the ship swung around behind the Moon. Down, it sank, and down, until the fantastic, jagged peaks silhouetted on the horizon seemed biting into it like gigantic fangs. Then it was gone, and the *Frontier* was on the side of the Moon never seen from Earth.

Dall's pulses were racing; if there were anything on the Moon, it would be here, where it would be safe from the prying eyes of Earth's huge telescopes. He glanced at Frontenac; the other's dark eyes were gleaming, as though in reflection of his own eagerness. Raising his heavily gloved hands to his helmet lenses in an illustrative gesture, Frontenac unfastened his straps and left the control room. He returned shortly with a pair of binoculars equipped with special light filters, and proceeded to scan intently the vast panorama below.

As Frontenac watched, the *Frontier* swept over the Moon's day side and began entering the Sunset zone. The ship was now closer to the surface; the sharp division between light and shadow was not as apparent as from higher above. Details of the airless, desolate little world now became vividly and almost startlingly clear; for the first time the mountainous irregularities of its surface became evident. Great craters, towering, fanged spires and ridges, and vast, sprawling serpentine chasms and gorges scarred and pitted the entire terrain. The shadows, which stretched from or filled them, showed plainly their enormous heights and depths.

THE shadows lengthened, and then the ship was suddenly on the Moon's night side, sweeping around toward the Sunrise zone. Dall and Frontenac stared at each other in mute, over-whelming despair. They had seen huge craters, mountainous ridges, and deep canyons; bizarre and unearthly, awe inspiring—but not greatly different from like features to be found on the Earthward side. There had been nothing on the eternally hidden side of the Moon to indicate the presence of human beings.

Dall sagged in utter defeat. Nothing. The entire Moon was dead and uninhabited after all.

He felt Frontenac touch his arm; saw him beckon and incline his head forward. He touched his helmet to that of the other in response.

"Looks like this is it, Harvey," Frontenac said. "Those meteorites had our names on them."

"I guess so," Dall answered dully. "The only hope we had of living beyond our remaining air supply is gone. There's nothing to show that people might somehow be living here."

Frontenac was silent a moment; then: "Harvey, did you have any theory at all of what we might find?"

"In a way. I remembered a while back that Melgard mentioned a place called Lunapolis. It might have been just a gag—but on the other hand, Melgard might have been referring to an actual base or camp on the Moon."

"In other words, you had the idea there might be some sort of surface settlement?"

"Something like that—though a settlement on the Moon's airless surface, alternately baked in terrific heat and frozen in terrific cold, seemed too fantastic to consider." Dall abruptly stiffened. "Jules! A surface settlement may be impossible—but what about a sub-surface or subterranean settlement?"

Frontenac gripped Dall's arm tensely. His tones were shrill with excitement. "I think you hit on something, Harvey! That might be the very answer."

"A subterranean settlement or base will be mighty hard to find," Dall pointed out. "But it'll have to have a surface entrance of some kind, and if there is one, we'll find it."

The utter darkness of the night side began brightening as the *Frontier* reached the Sunrise zone. Tendrils of flame that grew steadily in size danced on the Moon's serrated horizon. These emanated from the Sun's corona, where continuous, inconceivably violent explosions of blazing hydrogen rose and fell like the furiously storm-lashed waves of an immense, supernally flaming sea. Then the full vast orb of the Sun rose into view, a spectacle of awesome, breathtaking magnificence.

WHEN the hidden side of the Moon had once more been reached, Dall dropped the ship still closer to the surface. Then he balanced it on its jets, so that it ceased to fall and floated gently at a constant height and speed. The maneuver was enormously fuel wasting, but with no hope of regaining Earth on their diminished air supply, it was fuel that could be considered expendable.

With the binoculars, Frontenac narrowly probed the surface. Time passed as the ship crept along; shadows began to lengthen again as it moved toward the Sunset zone.

Frontenac became suddenly rigid; the binoculars dropped from his hands; and then, trembling visibly, his dark eyes were wide and incredulous behind their helmet lenses, he was pointing through the pilot shell. Surprised and puzzled, Dall turned his head to follow the direction of Frontenac's gloved finger; the ship's stern was pointed at the surface and Dall had in effect been riding backward. Now he saw what had whipped Frontenac to such a pitch of feverish excitement.

A city.

Dall stared in numbed, utter astonishment. A city! Tiny with distance, it was, yet obviously of large size, shining with alabaster whiteness in the Sun's rays. In the surrounding airlessness, its details stood out with vivid clarity. From the clustered buildings at its base numerous slender towers rose; one in particular, located approximately at the city's center, leaped upward to a surprising height. A complex network of aerial spans threaded among and through the buildings, emphasizing the futuristic aspect of their architecture. The city seemed like nothing so much as a city of Earth's future, somehow transported bodily through time and space, to the Moon.

Dall saw—but his mind rejected the evidence of his eyes. He must, he told himself, be the victim of a mirage caused in some fashion by the heat and brilliance of the Sun; or perhaps he was suffering from delusions brought on by the intense mental and physical strain of the past several hours. But it was apparent that Frontenac saw the city also; which meant that it must actually be there, since it was highly improbable that Frontenac could have been affected in exactly the same manner as Dall. Peering at the city more closely, Dall had to admit that it was too substantial and clear-cut to be a mirage or a delusion.

The city existed—it was real. But it had been nowhere in evidence the first time the *Frontier* passed this way. How had it materialized?

Within seconds Dall had the answer. The city, he saw, was mounted upon a circular column or base that rose from the throat of an enormous crater, fitting it as precisely as a piston fits its cylinder. And as a piston may be raised or lowered within its enclosing cylinder, so, Dall decided, could the column upon which the city stood be raised or lowered within the crater's throat. It was an effective and ingenious method for concealing the city from view; lowered within its shaft, the shadows filling the crater's mouth would render it almost completely invisible. Dall recalled having noticed the remarkable size of the crater, during the first search, but he had seen nothing to indicate that something might be hidden inside.

Thoughts whirled chaotically in Dall's mind. Why had the city been raised into sight, revealing its existence? Considering his and Frontenac's presence nearby, did the event have some special significance? Or was it merely accidental? For that matter, what was the city doing here, on the Moon? What was its purpose? Who were its inhabitants?

Dall concentrated the full power of his faculties upon that last question. *Who were the city's inhabitants? They,* the mysterious organization of which Melgard was an agent? If so it meant that *They* were possessed of greater abilities than Dall had ever realized. It meant that *They* had among its members master architects and engineers—men who scientifically were so far in advance of their contemporaries as to make them seem like throwbacks to the Stone Age.

DALL wondered abruptly if he weren't wrong in thinking about men—about human beings like himself. Perhaps it wasn't men who had built the city, but people of another race entirely; a race that had come from some far-off system, to build for some unknown purpose an outpost on the Moon.

The speculation sent an icy chill through Dall. An alien race from some incalculably remote world; grotesque, possibly utterly inhuman, in appearance. What would their purpose be in constructing a city on the Moon? As a military base in which to plan and prepare for war?

And Melgard—how did he fit in? Was he an ally of these hypothetical aliens, selling his own race down the river?

Melgard, Dall remembered again, had mentioned a place called Lunapolis. This seemed to be the name for the city at which Dall now peered. But who—or what—was the Phrenarch of Lunapolis?

Dall ceased his brooding conjectures as Frontenac turned away suddenly from a long and intent scrutiny of the fairy-like metropolis below. Beckoning, Frontenac leaned his helmeted head forward, and Dall brought his own helmet into contact.

"We've certainly stumbled onto something, Harvey. Wish I knew what to make of it; I expected something entirely different."

"I know," Dall said. "It's as though we'd been searching for a flea and found an elephant. I've just about blown a fuse trying to reason it out."

"Anyway, Harvey, the city's in line with what we were looking for—a place with air. What do we do now? My suggestion would be to fly right in and make ourselves at home."

"That tallies with my own ideas," Dall admitted. "No use being cagey; we'd have to land sooner or later. And besides, getting into the city seems the only way to find out certain things that are bothering me. So hold onto your helmet—here we go!"

Dall turned to the controls and began jockeying the *Frontier* over the city. It was an enormously difficult task, a space vessel being anything but maneuverable in a gravitational pull. But by dint of infinite patience and a staggering amount of consumed fuel, he accomplished it; the ship finally was hovering directly over the city.

Dall paused a moment, glancing downward, as he prepared to send the *Frontier* dropping. His gaze was caught and held by a number of brightly glinting motes that appeared suddenly from the metropolis below. They were in motion, rising swiftly upward. In another few seconds Dall realized what they were— ships. Four of them.

And then he recalled something else; the design of the oncoming craft was familiar. They were silver projectiles, slim and cigar-shaped, without tubes or fins—silver projectiles in every way identical to the one in which, back on the distant Earth, Melgard had attacked Dall and Frontenac.

The gleaming, sleek ships were hurtling up directly at the *Frontier.* Within them, Dall knew, were the minions of *They*— men or *things*—who had been pledged to the destruction of all Earthly craft.

CHAPTER NINE

ESCAPE was out of the question, having already had an experience with one of them, Dall was aware that he could not hope to elude the swift, agile vessels now approaching; and further it was necessary, considering the loss of their air supply, that he and Frontenac take refuge in the city. Yet he could not take the risk that the four oncoming ships intended the immediate annihilation of the *Frontier* and its passengers. Somehow he had to make a play for time. Once in the city, it was possible that he and Frontenac could indefinitely stall off death.

There was only one solution that Dall could see. He didn't hesitate; his hands began moving desperately over the controls. The *Frontier* dropped with reckless speed toward the toy-like expanse of the city below.

The four projectiles were taken completely by surprise; they evidently had expected the rocket to do anything but what it did just then. The momentum of their swift rush upward carried them past their prey and on into the distance. The gap increased still further as the *Frontier* steadily and rapidly descended.

Cold and tense, Dall watched the city grow in size and detail, spreading out and up like some enormously huge, swift-growing flower. At intervals he darted quick, comprehensive glances back at the projectiles. Belatedly they turned and came plummeting down in pursuit. When they had flashed by moments before, Dall had noticed something that he hadn't seen on Melgard's craft during the encounter over the lake; slim tubes had projected from the bows and sides of the four ships—weapons of some sort. Dall was thinking of this now as they came darting after the *Frontier*. In the confusion resulting from the speed and unexpectedness of Dall's ship-dropping strategy, he and Frontenac had not been fired at. But their momentary advantage was now gone.

The tip of the city's dominating central spire grew near. Dall felt a sudden, brief tingling shock, as though a mild electric current had passed through him. Frontenac's startled eyes showed that he had felt it, too. An invisible energy field of some sort, Dall decided; a field that quite probably enclosed the entire city within its zone of influence.

The gap between the *Frontier* and its pursuers was rapidly narrowing. But nothing issued as yet from the tube-weapons of the projectiles. The reason wasn't hard for Dall to guess. The *Frontier* was too close to the city; a miss would be certain to cause serious damage among the buildings.

Peering down, Dall saw a large rectangular clearing near the base of the central tower, which was now almost on a level with the ship. The clearing seemed to be a landing field, for the sleek, silver shapes of several projectiles rested at various places about the margin of it. Dall maneuvered the rocket toward the clearing, increasing the force of the blast to break its fall.

THE rectangle swelled in size; its smooth concrete surface came up, nearer and nearer; and then the blast touched, geysering up around the rocket. The way it did so revealed an astonishing fact to Dall—the city apparently was filled with air. Recalling the tingling shock that he had felt, he decided that the purpose of the energy field causing it was to prevent the air from leaking out into space. In effect the field was like a vast dome enclosing the city; it acted most likely by repelling the air molecules that tried to get through it.

Then a heavy shock went through the *Frontier,* announcing that it had touched ground. An instant later there was another shock as it settled, by virtue of its stern design, to a horizontal keel.

Dall cut the blast. He could see nothing immediately of his and Frontenac's new surroundings; steam rose in great clouds from a large, roughly circular area around the ship, where the terrific heat of the blast had blackened, cracked and pitted the concrete floor of the field.

Within his helmet, Dall's lips formed in a tight grin. So far, so good. He and Frontenac almost certainly wouldn't be so fortunate in what lay ahead—but at least they had this much to their credit. They had penetrated into the enemy's home base without a single shot having been fired.

Gradually the thick veils of ascending steam about the ship thinned and faded. Still nothing outside could be seen; the pilot shell was heavily fogged over, rivulets of moisture rolling down its smooth, sloping sides. Dall's helmet lenses, too, were clouded from the air and warmth that had rushed into the ship through the holes in its metal skin.

With a gesture for Frontenac to do likewise, Dall removed his helmet. He breathed deeply of the fresher, but burned-smelling air that now filled the control room. It was like nectar to his lungs; the air within his helmet had reached a dangerous point of deviation.

"Well, Harvey, here we are," were Frontenac's first words. "It seems we have the air situation well in hand—but there's one thing I'd like right now, and that's food. Wonder if the people here follow the time-honored custom of allowing the condemned a hearty meal?"

"Not if they're the kind of people I think they are," Dall said. "But it won't do any harm to find out." He unfastened his safety straps and stood up, stretching stiff, sore muscles. "Well, we'd better go out and pay our respects to our new hosts," he told Frontenac. "If we don't, they'll probably come in after us with cutting torches."

They left the control room. Dall unsealed the entrance hatch and pushed it open. A flood of warm, fragrant air poured in. Gripped by a sensation of eerie wonder, Dall glanced tensely about the portion of the landing field visible to him. Within minutes or scant seconds he would be face to face with the unknown inhabitants of this incredible city on the Moon. What would they be like? Monstrous, bizarre creatures, rivaling even the most dream-distorted figments of the wildest nightmare?

THEN, on the field directly opposite the *Frontier,* he saw a compact group of figures. Men, Dall realized, with a feeling that was almost relief. Men like himself—not grotesque aliens. The group stood between two of the silver projectiles, which Dall couldn't recall having previously been in that position on the field. He decided that the ships were part of those that had pursued Frontenac and him, having followed them down to the field. He didn't miss the fact that the tube weapons of the projectiles were pointed steadily at the *Frontier.* The other two ships, he guessed, would be on the other side of the rocket, doing likewise.

The group of men was very still; they seemed to be absorbed in an intent scrutiny of the *Frontier.* It was as though they expected something momentarily to happen.

Dall glanced at Frontenac. "Here goes," he said quietly. Raising his hands as a sign of surrender, he jumped from the hatch. He noted that his weight seemed as it would normally have been on Earth, and decided that the city was somehow provided with artificial gravity. In another second Frontenac joined him. They stood with raised hands, waiting for what would happen next.

A voice lifted in a barked command; men appeared magically from all about the field—men wearing strange, trim military uniforms and carrying automatic rifles. Quickly, and with a neat, machine-like precision, they surrounded the rocket and the two who stood before it. As one, they watched their prisoners in silent, grim-faced menace, weapons held alertly at the ready.

A wave of amazement broke over Dall. *Soldiers!* Soldiers…in a great and splendid city on the Moon! For what purpose had they been gathered and trained? For protection— or for war?

They all were young, he noted, clean-cut and intelligent in appearance, in the very prime of straight-bodied, firm muscled manhood. All were garbed in well-fitting, gray and blue uniforms, which consisted of a short tunic and loose trousers whose ends were gathered into the tops of ankle-high boots. Completing the uniforms were thick, white flare-brimmed helmets, with fitted-in visors of dark glass or plastic, apparently worn as protection against the heat and brilliance of the Sun— intense, even though the city was at present on the fringe of the Sunset zone.

For long seconds there was a deep, strained silence. Then footsteps became audible; they were approaching, and seemed to be made by a group of men. The ring of soldiers before Dall and Frontenac parted; five officers whose gray and blue uniforms bore unfamiliar rank insignia strode into the space between.

Dall's eyes narrowed abruptly in burning, intense interest. One of the officers was Bruce Melgard.

AT SIGHT of Dall and Frontenac, Melgard stopped short, dismayed surprise twisting his bluntly handsome face. There was a dim suggestion of superstitious terror about his reaction, like that of one who has seen a ghost. In another moment, however, he got himself under control; his square mouth hardened, and a sullen rage flared into his blue eyes. He said slowly, with rigid, icy self-control:

"So you managed somehow to escape from the flitterjet, eh? I thought it seemed too easy."

Dall shrugged deprecatingly. "I can hardly be blamed for trying; I dislike the idea of being smashed to mince meat as much as anyone."

"Well, you made a big mistake in coming to Lunapolis," Melgard grunted. "You won't be so lucky this time." He turned to the four men at his side. "Gentlemen, this is Harvey Dall, designer of the rocket that you now see; and this, Jules Frontenac, who supplied the construction funds. I realize that their presence here reflects discredit on me, but the failure of my mission was due to a circumstance beyond my control. Dall ate the drugged food along with the rest of the men, but for some reason he didn't go under. Everything that subsequently happened stems from this one fact."

The four men nodded and gazed at Dall in various degrees of interest. They were of a type, hard-featured, stiffly erect in carriage, and exuding a quality of cold, self-assured arrogance.

Melgard returned his attention to Dall. "There's only one explanation for the apparent failure of the drug to take hold on you—you must have been revived by someone."

Dall kept his face impassive. He'd long suspected Melgard of being more than ordinarily clever; he decided now the man was not only that, but uncannily shrewd as well. Again he had the disturbing impression that there was something odd about Melgard, and he wondered why this should be.

Melgard's hostile blue eyes had narrowed. "Thinking about it, Dall, I'm quite certain that someone did revive you. Who was it?"

Dall shook his head. "Sorry; it so happens that I don't know what you're talking about." Something that might have been instinct warned Dall to say nothing about the white-haired man. The stranger was an ally; revealing his identity, or even so much as the fact of his existence, might place him in danger—a poor reward for his aid. Dall went on, "All I know is that I got sick shortly after eating the food; almost lost consciousness. I realized something must have been wrong with the food, and forced myself to throw it up. Then I lay down for a while, and soon felt better."

Melgard looked doubtful. "That might be true—but I've had the strange feeling that someone else—" He broke off abruptly, shrugging his heavy shoulders. He turned once more to the four uniformed men beside him. "Dall is dangerous; his escapes both times prove that. And he and Frontenac can't be kept here as prisoners indefinitely. We would be foolish to take the risk that they might eventually find a way to warn Earth of our plans. I move that they both be executed at once."

His companions glanced at each other in evident unease. One of them spoke cautiously.

"But, General, the Phrenarch wouldn't approve—"

MELGARD gestured impatiently, sudden anger clouding his face. Then he grew grimly calm; his voice, when he answered, was lowered to a confidential tone that was barely audible to Dall, and which certainly must have been inaudible to the soldiers beyond. "The presence here of Dall and Frontenac demonstrates clearly that the Phrenarch's policies are impractical. I advocated more outright measures in Dall's particular case, but the Phrenarch insisted that I follow the standard procedure. This is the result. If Dall's rocket hadn't descended within the range of our detectors, we'd never have known he was still alive until too late. He'd have returned to Earth. He wouldn't have known about Lunapolis, of course, since we'd raised into sight only after the detector alarms went off, so we could send out pursuit ships; but if he'd returned, our whole campaign against Earth's rocket research would have been destroyed at one blow."

The four nodded thoughtfully. Melgard resumed, following up a clearly evident advantage; his voice was still low, but underscored now by a note of insistence.

"The conquest of an entire world is anything but an easy one; the task facing us it not only immense, but enormously difficult. As soldiers we know success can be achieved only through a sternly realistic attitude. Wars aren't won by gentle measures; the Phrenarch's idealistic concepts are inconsistent—doomed to failure. Continuing to follow them might very well mean the loss of everything we've worked for."

The four men nodded again. It was apparent to Dall that they were being won over. He knew what was taking place: for some reason the Phrenarch—whoever that was—wouldn't approve of an execution; Melgard was using this as one reason for urging a revolt. If he won, Dall realized, the deaths of Frontenac and himself would swiftly follow.

Melgard went on eagerly, "We five compose the Military Council. The majority of the troops will obey our orders without question once they understand the issues at stake. We could take over Lunapolis within an hour. Gentlemen,"— Melgard straightened with urgent purpose in his bearing—"it is now or never! What is your decision?"

The four momentarily hesitated. And while they did so, there rose into sudden audibility the clatter of swiftly approaching, metal-soled feet.

'Make way!" a voice cried. "Make way for the Phrenarch!"

Melgard and his confederates stiffened in guilty alarm. Licking his lips, a hunted, feral expression on his face, Melgard glanced quickly from Dall to the oncoming group. Dall met the other's look with a slow triumphant grin. Thwarted fury blazed into Melgard's eyes.

Dall realized abruptly why Melgard was so anxious to get him and Frontenac out of the way. Melgard had failed in his mission at the construction camp. His orders obviously had been to kidnap Dall and Frontenac, and to destroy or at least seriously damage the *Frontier*. It seemed evident that Dall and Frontenac were not to have been harmed, but kept where they would be unable to continue their rocket research. Melgard, however, had failed to wreck the *Frontier,* and in the case of Dall and Frontenac, he had attempted outright, cold-blooded murder. It was certain that he had lied to gloss over what had happened. Dall was thus now in a position to show that he had lied.

Melgard was in a difficult spot. And there was no time for him to do anything about it just then; the newcomers had already reached the gathering before the rocket.

Foremost was a figure in an enveloping cloak and hood, made of some silvery, reflecting material, which was obviously worn as protection against the intense Lunar Sun. Three men in civilian clothes and a guard of four soldiers followed.

"What is the meaning of this?" the person in the cloak demanded, in tones strangely soft yet coldly imperious. "Who are these men? How did their ship manage to reach the Moon?"

The face of the speaker turned momentarily toward Dall; he stared in blank incredulity. The identity of the Phrenarch of Lunapolis came to him as a complete, devastating surprise.

For the Phrenarch was—*a girl!*

CHAPTER TEN

BELATEDLY Melgard and his four companions lifted their arms in a salute. Melgard's face was now calm and controlled. He said quietly:

"These men, Leader, are Harvey Dall and Jules Frontenac."

The girl stiffened perceptibly; she glanced once more at Dall. Her eyes, a clear, vivid emerald green, were startled and intense. Dall returned her gaze woodenly. She was, he decided, undeniably attractive, though a bit too cold and arrogantly assured in expression to be termed beautiful.

Then, with a swift, comprehensive look at Frontenac, she turned back to Melgard. "I believe you told me that Dall and Frontenac died back on Earth in an attempt to crash your cruiser." Her tones were sarcastically accusing.

Melgard nodded with just the right touch of ruefulness. "That is what I thought, Leader. It now seems that the two must have jumped from their flitterjet instants before sending it at the cruiser. And since the flitterjet fell into the lake after the crash, there was no way to check up on what actually had happened."

Frontenac snorted and darted Dall a glance of amazement. Dall caught the girl's eyes and said:

"It seems that Melgard's story needs some serious corrections. We weren't the ones who tried to crash him; in a flitterjet that would have been suicidal. On the contrary, he's the one who crashed our ship. Frontenac and I escaped, of course, but the fact remains that Melgard tried to kill us."

Melgard said evenly, "It's General Melgard now, Dall—and don't you forget it."

The girl swung to him. "Is Dall telling the truth? I ordered him to be put out of the way, but not actually hurt. You know it's my policy in this campaign never knowingly to take a life."

Melgard shook his head, smiling slightly, as though in wonder. "Dall's a clever scoundrel; the time we were forced to spend on him proves that. It should be obvious, Leader, that he's trying to create an issue between us in the hope that it will give him and Frontenac a chance to escape."

"Nice going, General," Dall said, smiling thinly. "It's my word against yours—and you seem to be top dog around here."

Frontenac snorted again. "If the so innocent General didn't try his best to make hash out of us, then I've got several gray hairs that are going to be hard to account for."

Melgard drew himself up, frowning. In his uniform he made an impressive picture of annoyed dignity.

"Enough of this," the girl snapped abruptly, stern green eyes sweeping Dall and Frontenac. "I'll have no extemporaneous remarks, if you please. If you have anything to say, I would prefer it to be in answer to questions I have asked." She turned to Melgard. "Do you give me your word, General, that the story you have told me is completely true?"

"Of course, Leader." Melgard's manner was crisp and decisive, yet with a subtle shading of indignation. "Dall was merely trying to create a misunderstanding between us, and since you know nothing of his character, it's natural that you should be disturbed."

DALL raged inwardly, but he kept himself in tight control. He knew that any further efforts to refute Melgard would be useless. It was human nature that this girl who was known as the Phrenarch of Lunapolis should be more inclined to believe one of her own men rather than a complete stranger. But what made the situation completely exasperating was that, in so doing, she was unknowingly aiding Melgard in his traitorous plans for the overthrow of her authority. And with the girl out of the way, there would be nothing to prevent Melgard from executing Dall and Frontenac.

"Very well," the girl said. "One thing more, General. I selected you to deal personally with the Dall-Frontenac case, since a previous experience with Dall promised that there would be considerable difficulty. As you have explained, unforeseen complications prevented you from carrying out the mission as originally planned. It isn't my purpose to go into the matter again; the important thing is that a rocket has finally succeeded in leaving Earth—a fact which places our entire campaign in danger.

"Most probably Dall and Frontenac left secretly, but sooner or later the news will get out. We must repair the damage that will cause. There is only one way to do so; it must be made to appear that the rocket failed after all. This can be accomplished by fitting it with degravity units and towing it back to Earth. Then, when its original departure point has been reached, it can be exploded by remote control, to make it seems as though the rocket had blown up in landing. Since little or nothing will be left of it afterward, the natural assumption will be made that Dall and Frontenac were inside. This must be done at night; and care be taken that witnesses aren't killed in the blast."

Melgard nodded in approval. "An excellent plan, Leader. I shall see that a special detail is put to work on it."

"You evidently misunderstood me, General," the girl said incisively. "You are personally to take charge of this matter. And at once."

"But I've practically just arrived in Lunapolis," Melgard protested. "After having been away so long—"

The Phrenarch cut in sharply, "The rocket is your responsibility, General! It wouldn't be here if you hadn't failed in your mission. If you wish to avoid what is clearly a continuation of your original duty, I shall be forced to relieve you of your post. I am sure that one or more of your subordinates would be eager for the chance to succeed you."

She glanced at the four officers standing stiffly at attention behind Melgard. All were covertly but quite plainly interested.

Melgard's blunt features were mask-like, but a malevolent gleam showed in his eyes. He bowed slightly and said, "Perhaps I have jumped to conclusions, Leader. I shall, of course, take charge of the rocket matter immediately."

THE girl nodded. "Very well. As for Dall and Frontenac, they will be lodged temporarily in Capitol Tower, until psychologists determine their respective aptitudes for work other than rocketry. Since they are in Lunapolis, they might as well make themselves useful."

"Work?" Frontenac exclaimed. He jabbed his chest with a thumb in a fierce gesture of outrage. "I, Jules Frontenac—*work?* Why, my dear young lady—"

"Phrenarch is the correct title of address, if you please," the girl interrupted. "And as for working, work you most assuredly shall. You're not on Earth anymore, as you know."

"I certainly wish I was," Frontenac growled.

"It may not be so bad, Jules," Dall said comfortingly. "They're going to find our aptitudes, you know. That means we might even be dumb enough to become generals like Melgard."

"That will do!" The Phrenarch's attractive features were stern, but for an instant it seemed that amusement danced in her vivid green eyes. She turned and began issuing crisp orders to the assemblage about her. Then, gathering her silver cloak, and followed by the three men in civilian clothes—who, from their elderly, scholarly appearances, seemed cabinet members or advisers—she strode away.

The Phrenarch's four personal guards ranged themselves around Dall and Frontenac, and the two were ordered curtly into motion. Dall turned for a last glance at Melgard. The General's face, he saw, wore a most unpleasant expression of baffled fury.

Capitol Tower, Dall found, was the dominating central spire, which he had earlier noticed while landing in the *Frontier.* He saw the Phrenarch and her three escorts disappear into the huge, ornate entrance, and a short time later he and Frontenac were marched inside. He found himself in an immense, brightly-lighted, and luxuriously beautiful lobby, lined at one end by banks of elevators. Followed closely by their guards, he and Frontenac were guided into one of the elevators, and the car shot smoothly up. They emerged at last into a long, high-arched hall, studded with doors at regular intervals that had the appearance of a hotel or dormitory hall. A walk took them through a series of other halls, and presently they were ushered into a large room.

Dall turned to one of the guards, who, he had noticed, seemed to be the leader. "Say, mind telling me a few things? Who built this city? What's going on here?"

"Sorry," the guard said. "I'm not allowed to answer questions."

"Maybe there's one you can," Dall persisted. "For example, what's the name of this female who calls herself the Phrenarch?"

The guard grinned briefly. "Ellen Pancrest. But you might as well forget she's a female; she's colder than an iceberg and about as dangerous to fool with as a tiger."

"Pancrest," Dall mused. "Pancrest... Seems I've heard or read the name somewhere..."

THE guard shrugged. "Just remember a few things. It's no use making a break, so stay right here. We'll be right outside the door. If you want anything—"

"Food," Frontenac said abruptly. "I want food—lots of it."

"Check." The guards left, and the door clicked shut.

Dall snapped his fingers. "I've got it!"

"Got what?" Frontenac asked. "Oh—the name?"

"Yes—it's Lloyd Pancrest. Read about him in a book or something like that. He was an inventor—a genius; he made at least several fortunes from his discoveries. He worked on a lot of things, rockets among them. This was over twenty years ago, and if anyone could have turned out a successful rocket back at that time, Lloyd Pancrest would have been the man to do it. But for some reason he suddenly gave up inventing and started a cult."

"What?" Frontenac frowned in disbelief. "A cult?"

"Something like that," Dall said. "It was a sort of social or political movement. The name…wait a minute. It began with an F, I think. Friends…? No, more like Phrenarch." Abruptly Dall stiffened. "That's it; that's the name! Phrenarchy!"

"Phrenarch…phrenarchy," Frontenac muttered. "Look, Harvey, what happened to this Lloyd Pancrest?"

"I don't know; my source of information didn't seem to mention that. He must have faded into gradual obscurity, I guess."

"On the other hand, Harvey, he could have taken his whole Phrenarchy cult to the Moon."

"Of course! Phrenarch Ellen Pancrest of Lunapolis—and Lloyd Pancrest, founder of Phrenarchy. More than a coincidence there… Jules, that's probably just what Lloyd Pancrest did—took his whole Phrenarchy cult here, to the Moon! Secretly. And he must have invented a rocket after all—or something just as good as a rocket…also secretly."

"The ships they have here, Harvey! Cruisers, the girl called them. Ships without rockets; ships that move by some unknown means of propulsion."

"Maybe not unknown at that," Dall pointed out. "Back on Earth, I guessed that Melgard's ship utilized gravity or gravitic lines of force. And you'll recall that the girl—Ellen Pancrest—mentioned degravity units, or something like that."

Dall fell to pacing the floor, forehead creased in thought. Muttered words fell in his wake.

"Twenty years ago…a scientific genius named Lloyd Pancrest, and a cult or movement called Phrenarchy. Today…a splendid city on the hidden side of the Moon, and a girl named Ellen Pancrest, who calls herself the Phrenarch. Twenty years…"

Frontenac said softly, in wonder, "And in that time, Harvey, they built this city."

"It's hard to believe. Lloyd Pancrest was a genius, true enough, but a city like this couldn't possibly be the product of one man's genius. It would take an army of geniuses to do it in twenty years. And to assume that Lloyd Pancrest's cult was both the size of an army and composed entirely of geniuses, is far too much."

"But the city's here, Harvey."

DALL ceased his pacing; he nodded, metal-gray eyes narrowed intently. "Yes, it's here, all right. And we know that its inhabitants have gone through a lot of trouble to keep the people of Earth from learning that it's here. That's the main idea behind the secret sabotaging of Earth's rocket progress. These Phrenarchists—or whatever they call themselves—have been so infernally clever and efficient about it, in fact, that nobody on Earth knows exactly what is happening. Even men like Merrick and Weston have nothing to work on but a lot of wild guesses."

"We got past them," Frontenac pointed out. "We reached the Moon."

Dall shrugged. "Mainly through a combination of imponderables and just plain luck, that couldn't happen again in a hundred years. If the white-haired stranger hadn't showed up when he did, things would have turned out otherwise."

"The white-haired stranger!" Frontenac was suddenly eager. "Harvey, he knew what was going to happen back at camp; he seems to know everything that's going on. Maybe he knows we're here; maybe he'll be good enough to help us again."

"Even if he knows we're here," Dall said, "I don't see how he'd reach us. It's anything but a short walk to the Moon, you know. And Melgard seems to suspect that the stranger is some- where in the background. Melgard's shrewd—and devilishly clever. Back at camp I never thought he was anything other than a technician. He knew his job forward and back... You know, Jules, there's something odd about Melgard that I've noticed about the Phrenarchists, too."

Frontenac nodded slowly. "Now that you've mentioned it, I think I know what you mean. It's a sort of quickness they have…a sort of complete and vivid aliveness, as though they could do things at an instant's notice…and do it calmly, coldly, calculatingly. It hasn't struck me as remarkable, Harvey, because you have somewhat the same qualities yourself."

"Smile when you say that, pardner," Dall grinned. He quickly sobered. "Anyway, there's nothing wrong with the Phrenarchists; they're a smart and tricky bunch. As to what they're up to, it isn't hard to guess. Melgard mentioned war— the conquest of a world. That world can only be Earth. The Phrenarchists seem to be planning to take over; and, Jules, with the organization they have, with weapons like the cruisers, don't doubt for a second that they couldn't do it. It would be as easy as falling off a log."

CHAPTER ELEVEN

THERE was a sudden clicking noise; the door opened. A uniformed guard bearing a dish-laden tray strode into the room. He deposited his burden upon a fragile-looking metal and plastic table and left. The door clicked shut again.

Frontenac eagerly inspected the contents of the tray. "Hm-m-m…smells good. And looks good."

"If you're just going to admire the stuff," Dall said, "then get out of the way for a man who wants to eat."

Later Dall began an examination of his and Frontenac's new quarters. A door at one side of the room, about which he'd developed a strong curiosity, proved to lead into a large bedchamber. There were two more doors here, one leading into a glittering tile and chrome bath, and the other into a closet, which was empty. The furnishings of the two main rooms were simple yet comfortable, exhibiting in their design the same futuristic effect that Dall earlier had noticed about the city itself.

Examination of the bathroom had showed it to be completely equipped with shaving and bath accessories. Dall and Frontenac took quick advantage of the opportunity to freshen up.

Afterward time began to lag. There was a well-stocked recessed bookcase in the living room, but Dall and Frontenac were too tense to read. Both were filled with chaotically mingled sensations of curiosity, anticipation, and unease. They talked little, and either sat and smoked in strained, brooding silence, or took turns at restlessly pacing the floor.

They began to yawn—a tendency that gradually grew too pronounced to ignore.

"Might as well get some sleep," Dall said at last. "They'll get around to us sooner or later, I guess."

When Dall awoke, he found that Frontenac was already up. A guard brought in a breakfast tray as he finished dressing and went into the living room. The meal was followed by another period of restless waiting.

And then the door unceremoniously clicked open. A squad of four guards was revealed. The squad obviously was a relief shift, for the faces of the men were unfamiliar. Their leader advanced a few steps into the room and said:

"All right, come along."

Dall stood up slowly from the chair in which he had been sitting. "Where to?"

"You'll find out when you get there," the guard said.

Dall shrugged, controlling his exasperation with an effort. He was joined by Frontenac, and with guards in their fore and rear, they were led to their mysterious destination. An elevator ride took them to a still higher floor of Capitol Tower. They emerged into a vast hall that was as luxurious and imposing in its futuristic way as the hall of a palace. A certainty grew in Dall's mind as he peered about him—it was possible that he and Frontenac were being taken to Ellen Pancrest. Only a person as high in authority as the Phrenarch would live in such surroundings.

HIS surmise proved to be right; a pair of inlaid metal doors at the end of the hall gave into a huge room, where Ellen Pancrest sat behind a great semi-circular desk.

She was not alone, Dall saw; several men in civilian clothes stood quietly a short distance away, in front and to one side of the desk. Across from the men were two chairs, which had been fitted up with scientific apparatus of some sort.

An alarm bell jangled in Dall's mind. Those chairs... What was Ellen Pancrest planning to do?

The girl was smoking a cigarette; she used it to gesture with when Dall and Frontenac had been escorted up to the chairs. "That will be all," she told the guards, in her cool imperious voice. "You may withdraw."

The guards saluted in unison. Dall was only dimly aware of them as they left; he was gazing intently at Ellen Pancrest. Divested now of her silvery cloak and hood, she was somehow a different person. Her hair was a light brown, with undertones of deep gold. It was piled atop her small head in thick curls. She wore a mannish plain gray suit over a silk blouse of canary yellow. Her only jewelry was a large turquoise brooch pinned to her suit. There was a subtle polished perfection about her, and yet the sort of simplicity that marks one of exquisitely cultured tastes.

Dall noted that her expression, too, had undergone a change; it was no longer cold and arrogant. Her face seemed lighted from within by a flame of something that seemed an intense, burning purpose. It made her more completely feminine—and, Dall reluctantly had to admit, even beautiful.

The vivid green eyes lifted momentarily to Dall and passed on to Frontenac. A slim white hand waved its cigarette in a gesture toward the two chairs.

"Won't you sit down?" Ellen Pancrest invited.

Dall smiled thinly. "Said the lady spider to the two male flies. Just what have you got there—improved versions of the electric chairs they use on Earth?"

A trace of sardonic amusement showed on the girl's red lips, and then was gone. "I assure you, Mr. Dall, that you won't be harmed. I merely wish to ask a few questions, and to…facilitate matters, the chairs have been equipped with lie detectors. These are of a new and advanced type, which is perhaps why you didn't recognize them for what they were."

"I see…" Dall glanced thoughtfully at the chairs and then back to the girl. "But I'm afraid I don't understand why you should need lie detectors. What sort of questions do you intend to ask?"

"You'll find out once you sit down, Mr. Dall."

"Look here, this lie detector business isn't entirely necessary, you know. Jules and I will promise to answer your questions truthfully."

The green eyes hardened. "I'll be certain you're answering truthfully only when the lie detectors are checking on you. Now sit down, or I'll summon the guards to see that you do."

DALL shrugged with outward unconcern, though inwardly he was tense. If the girl suspected he was connected with the Secret Service, the lie detectors might very likely divulge the fact, despite his denials. And once she knew the truth about him, the girl would be certain to take precautions, which would destroy his already frail hopes of eventually somehow making an escape.

Turning to Frontenac, Dall gestured elaborately toward the chairs. "After you, my dear Gaston."

But Frontenac was equally polite. "No, no, my dear Alphonse, after you. I insist."

Dall bowed. "Your kindness touches me—like a pain in the neck."

Ellen Pancrest hid her grin behind a cloud of cigarette smoke as the two marched in mock solemnity to the chairs and sat down. The technicians immediately became busy over them, fastening metal bands about their wrists and foreheads. Finally it was done; one of the technicians spoke to the girl, appraising her of the fact, while the others turned to a control cabinet nearby.

Deliberately, Ellen Pancrest crushed out her cigarette and leaned forward at the desk. "Mr. Dall, you said something a while back that interested me very much. You were referring, if you will recall, to an alleged attempt made by General Melgard back on Earth, to take your life, and that of Mr. Frontenac. You insisted that it was his cruiser and not your flitterjet that had tried to crash the other party involved. Now...is this true?"

"It's true, all right," Dall said.

"Of course," Frontenac growled.

The girl glanced at the technicians, who were watching intently two slowly revolving paper cylinders within the cabinet. A line was being drawn upon each of the cylinders by an inked stylus. The cylinders were ruled with lines according to some form of a graph, each line being designated by letters and numbers in an unfamiliar system of symbols.

The technician who earlier had announced the readiness of the test met the girl's questioning gaze and nodded. He seemed to be in charge of the group. He said:

"Complete truth is indicated, Leader."

Nothing moved in Ellen Pancrest's face. She studied the desktop a moment, sitting very quietly. Then she glanced once more at Dall.

"I'm curious, Mr. Dall. Just what did happen back on Earth between you and General Melgard? To be more precise, how did you manage to defeat his plans so thoroughly? Start at the beginning, if you please. I believe the beginning of the affair was when General Melgard's partner on the mission, Colonel Hartley, drugged the food served at a meal earlier on the same day. I'm particularly interested in how you succeeded in throwing off the effects of the drug."

Dall thought swiftly. If at all possible, he wanted to avoid implicating the white-haired man. The mysterious stranger might very well be an ace in the hole as regarded plans for an escape. And Dall owed the other a debt of gratitude, which precluded endangering him.

Just how efficient was the lie detector anyway? Dall decided to find out. He said:

"Getting around the drug wasn't so hard. When I felt it taking hold, I guessed what was wrong and forced myself to throw up everything I'd eaten. I felt sick and dizzy for a while, but it wasn't long before I returned to normal."

AS HE spoke he concentrated fiercely in an effort to convince himself that this actually had happened.

"The statement has been indicated as completely false, Leader," the head technician said.

Ellen Pancrest said quietly, "You're trying to hide something, Mr. Dall. It seems that the way you overcame the drug is a lot more remarkable than that."

"All right," Dall said. "A man revived me."

"The statement is partially true, Leader."

"Who was this man, Mr. Dall?"

"I don't know who he was."

"Completely true, Leader."

"You don't know his name?"

"I don't know anything about him."

"Completely true, Leader."

The girl hesitated, green eyes narrowed in evident mystification. She took her lower lip between her teeth and gazed at Dall without seeming to see him. Then her eyes sharpened on Dall; she released her lip and said:

"Describe this man, Mr. Dall."

"I don't know what he looks like. It was too dark to make out any details of his appearance."

"The statement is completely false, Leader."

Ellen Pancrest stood up and walked slowly from behind the desk. She had a graceful, finely moulded figure that bespoke radiant health and a quick, supple strength unusual in a woman. Her face was cold and set, its actual beauty no longer quite so apparent. She came to a stop a few paces in front of Dall and said:

"You might be interested to know, Harvey Dall, that I'm being quite polite in using the lie detector on you. You already know how efficient it is. Well, my scientists have a truth serum that gives even better results—though it's somewhat drastic. So you'd better make up your mind to tell the truth, because I'll get the truth out of you either way."

Dall met the imperious green eyes with glinting metal-gray ones. Muscles at his angular jaws were bunched palely against the angry despair that beat through him. He spoke softly:

"You're much too used to having your own way. It's made you too big for your shoes. What you seem to need—and apparently what you never got—is a frequent good spanking."

"Indeed?" Ellen Pancrest drawled. "And no doubt you think you could give me one?"

"You hold the whip hand here—but call off your dogs for five minutes, and I'll show you whether or not I could."

"That isn't necessary; I'm sure you're quite a beast."

"At least I'm not a spoiled brat."

The girl's full lips thinned, and her strong lithe body tensed. She leaned forward slightly, the fingers of her right hand splaying as though imminently about to strike.

Dall's hands were on the arms of his chair, ridged tendons showing in sharp relief on the backs of them. His eyes were steady and very bright.

Faces twisted in alarm, the technicians started toward the pair.

Frontenac watched in breathless rigidity, apprehensive and eager.

THEN the girl relaxed, her green gaze lidding. She murmured, "If I were a man, Harvey Dall, I think I'd enjoy beating you to a pulp. Unfortunately I'm not. But I do, as you've said, hold the whip hand here. I want information out of you—and information I'm going to get. And I'm going to remember your defiance when it comes to assigning you work. It's obvious that you're very strong. Well, I'll see to it that you're given a job in proportion to your strength—hard labor, to be exact…very hard labor."

Dall said nothing. He watched balefully as Ellen Pancrest turned and strode back to the desk. She perched on the edge of it and lighted another cigarette. When she looked at Dall again, her face was calm and coldly remote. She said quietly:

"I want a description of the man who revived you, Mr. Dall. I'm not bluffing about the truth serum, of course. If you refuse to tell me what I want to know, the truth serum will get it out of you anyway. And I warn you the experience will not be pleasant."

Dall shrugged slightly, and began to describe the white-haired stranger. He kept his eyes fixed upon a huge window behind the girl. He didn't look at her until he finished.

"Complete truth is indicated, Leader," the head technician droned.

Ellen Pancrest seemed not to hear. She was staring intently into space, the cigarette smoldering, forgotten, between her rigid fingers.

Dall studied the girl a moment. She seemed to know something about the stranger. And her mood seemed to be one that offered an opportunity to obtain the answer to a mystery that had long bothered him. He asked:

"Do you know the man?"

"Not exactly," she said, still staring into space. "He was seen in Lunapolis a few times. He seemed to be a spy, but we were unable to apprehend him." She looked finally at Dall, green eyes narrowing. "He helped you, Harvey Dall. That means he's my enemy, and considering the fact that he seems able to travel between Earth and Moon, a very dangerous one. I don't know who's behind him or what he's up to—but I do know one thing: If he shows up in Lunapolis again, I'll be ready for him."

CHAPTER TWELVE

FOR a moment her green eyes blazed a deadly promise. Then the grimness left her face, and once more it was controlled and coldly remote. She drew at her cigarette, sent a plume of fragrant smoke curling toward the ceiling.

"My curiosity hasn't been satisfied yet, Mr. Dall. What happened after you were revived?"

Dall told of his encounter with Melgard while on the way to the hangar, to investigate the danger threatening the *Frontier*. He described the fight that had followed, and was about to tell of his killing the man whom the girl had called Colonel Hartley, when she raised a hand for silence. She glanced inquiringly at the head technician. The man nodded.

"Completely true, so far, Leader."

She was silent a moment, regarding Dall intently. Then she signaled for him to continue.

Dall completed his intention of explaining about Hartley's death. He finished, "It was self-defense, of course. Hartley would have killed me, if I hadn't got him first."

Ellen Pancrest shook her head slightly. "I'm sorry it had to happen. Colonel Hartley must have been badly confused to try killing you. He and General Melgard had orders to avoid taking lives. They were equipped to deal with emergencies in a less blood-thirsty way."

"They certainly didn't try," Dall said. "I don't think they intended to. And for that matter, there's more than a good chance that a lot of deaths, which Melgard explained as accidental, may have been outright murder."

"That has occurred to me—even if rather late."

"Fine. Now a little birdie is going to tell you something. Keep a close watch on Melgard. He doesn't like your policies.

He believes that direct action is the only way to win; and he's planning a revolt to take over Lunapolis."

The girl's red lips were formed in a smile of grim amusement. "The little bird hasn't told me anything I didn't already suspect. That's why I insisted on having Melgard return to Earth. I wanted a little time to prepare certain...defenses, we might say. Your rocket offered a convenient excuse to get him out of the way for a while." She gestured. "Go on with your story, please. What happened after the Colonel Hartley incident?"

Dall told of having bound Melgard, and of the latter's subsequent escape. He related his and Frontenac's pursuit in the flitterjet; pursuit that had resulted in a vicious attack upon the craft by the hidden cruiser in which Melgard had taken refuge. Detailing how he and Frontenac cheated death, he went on to sketch briefly the flight to the Moon, and the disaster caused by the meteorites that had forced them to land in Lunapolis.

He made a motion of finality. "You know the rest."

ELLEN PANCREST was gazing into distance. A deeply thoughtful expression softened the cold remoteness of her face; she was beautiful again. Finally she stood up and waved at the group of technicians.

"That's all. You may take your things and leave." She went around behind her desk and sat down. She became lost in the distance once more, as the technicians packed their equipment and strode quietly from the room.

Dall said, "Those men heard your plans concerning Melgard. One or more of them might be working for him, you know."

Ellen Pancrest shook her head with a faint impatience. "They're completely trustworthy I assure you. They wouldn't have been in a position to hear my remarks if they weren't."

"Where is Melgard? Still here?"

"No; he left for Earth a short time ago. I waited for him to leave before summoning you here." The girl paused a moment, then abruptly leaned forward at the desk. "Mr. Dall, certain things you've told me may require a complete change in my intentions regarding you."

Dall's forehead wrinkled. "What do you mean by that?"

"It's rather complicated," the girl said. "I'd have to start at the very beginning to explain it fully."

"An explanation is something I'd like to have," Dall said. "I know this much: You're related to a man named Lloyd Pancrest, who was a famous inventor over twenty years ago. Lloyd Pancrest gave up inventing to start a cult or movement called Phrenarchy. Then he faded into obscurity—or disappeared. Your name and title, and your presence here, on the Moon, seems to indicate that Lloyd Pancrest somehow brought part or all of his cult to the Moon." He gestured and said, "You might take it from there."

Ellen Pancrest's expression had softened still further. Her face now had a warm and vivid loveliness so striking that it was as though, for the moment, she were another personality entirely. She said slowly:

"Lloyd Pancrest was my father. He was more than an inventor; he was a genius who could have won wealth and fame in any field of endeavor he might have chosen. He preferred to be an inventor mainly because it was a profession that allowed him to work alone; that made it possible for him to avoid daily contact with others. You see, my father wasn't like ordinary men; he was…different. He was, to be precise, a mutant."

Dall stiffened. "A…what?"

"A mutant, Mr. Dall; an individual with characteristics differing from the norm of his species because of some sort of evolutionary change. This change may be large or small, and is usually an hereditary one in that it is transmissible to future generations. In the latter case, it may be dominant or recessive; and it may or may not have survival value.

"In my father's case, the change was basically one of degree rather than kind. He was not a true superman, though he did have characteristics superior to those of ordinary men. He was a true mutant, however; his change may have been small, but it was fundamentally important—important enough for him to be considered one of an entirely new species. The change was hereditary, and dominant; for as my father later found, the new species bred true to type in every generation. And the change did have survival value...a curiously appropriate kind."

ELLEN PANCREST paused reflectively. "Mr. Dall, has it ever occurred to you that Man, as he is today, is pitifully unsuited to the civilization he has built around himself?"

Dall was thoughtful. "In a dim sort of way, yes. But I won't lay claims to being a social philosopher; such opinions as I have about Man in relation to his environment are mostly second-hand. It's generally admitted, you know, that Man, socially, is far behind himself, scientifically."

The girl nodded. "Exactly. And the reason for this is that Man mentally is an anachronism. Modern existence has become too complex, subject to too many strains and difficulties. Man's mind had reached the limits of its capacity to adjust. When he adjusts at all, it is only to those immediate features or phases that fit his color, race, and creed. That's why Earth is torn by constantly recurring wars, by crime, by economic panics, and by an increasing amount of mental and moral degeneration.

"In addition, modern knowledge has advanced enormously in scope and detail. It has outstripped Man's capacity to learn. He learns slowly on the average, can absorb only a limited amount of general information, and is forced by time and the necessities of existence to confine himself to one specific and immediately practical subject. Thus we have the spectacle of a man who is a master of his own particular branch of training, but who has only a broad, general knowledge of other branches within the field, and who is abysmally ignorant of other, unallied fields."

Dall shrugged. "That's no more than natural; a man can't learn everything there is to know."

"Natural, according to the standards with which you are familiar," Ellen Pancrest said. "Unnatural, according to mine. You are aware of General Melgard's record during the work on your rocket, Mr. Dall. He passed himself off as a technician, and you'll have to admit that you never suspected he might have been anything else. He could have posed as a metallurgist or a rocket fuel chemist with equal success. My own father, as I've mentioned, could have made himself outstanding in any field he might have turned to. It's all due to an ability to learn more, with greater ease and rapidity; to concentrate more efficiently and remember more effectively; to start with the general and to go into the specific by a combination of logic and deduction.

"But to continue: Another feature of modern life is that it has become too swift—deadly swift. Man is out of gear with it. His brain and nervous system, his thought processes and neuro-muscular reflexes, have been unable to keep pace. Machines have speeded up; accident statistics on industry, on surface and air traffic, show the result. The whole pattern of living has speeded up; and statistics again show the result: A decline in the general health, an increase in mental and nervous disorders—psycho-neuroses, phobias, hysteria, and insanity."

THE girl shook her head slightly, as though in wonder and pity. "So we have a rather sad picture of present Man. He learns slowly—when he tries to learn at all; and the capacity of his mind is such that he can absorb only a small portion of the vast mass of existing knowledge. And what knowledge he does absorb, he is unable properly to integrate and utilize for the fullest advantage of himself and his fellows. Burden his mind too far with details and responsibilities, and it snaps under the strain. And where co-ordination between mind and muscle is concerned, he reacts too slowly to the speeds and dangers of city life. He has adjusted himself to city existence without actually being mentally or physically constituted for it. He is still a creature of the fields and forests—still a primitive, living in cities instead of caves, killing with atomic bombs instead of stones, and traveling in jet-propelled craft instead of swinging through the trees.

"What, then, would a more highly evolved type of man be like—a true city creature? For one thing, he would have an improved and more efficient brain; he would be able to learn easily and quickly, concentrate and remember more readily, and master a wide range of knowledge. He would be able to think faster and more clearly, and make instantaneous decisions. And he would have a more advanced and highly integrated type of nervous system. He would be able to perform extremely dangerous tasks without becoming involved in accidents; he would, if actually confronted with danger, be able to react in a hundredth of the time it takes an ordinary man to react. He would be emotionally stable, free of neuroses, hysteria, and general mental unbalance. He would be able to take on a greater amount of detail and responsibility, and deal with it longer, with little or no danger to his health and sanity.

"My father was such a man. He was a new type of man without being actually a superman. He wasn't telepathic or clairvoyant; he didn't have any strange organs or senses. What he did have was complete adjustment to his environment, a higher degree of survival value. He was a perfect city creature, as ordinary men originally were perfect forest creatures. But he was different enough for others to be aware of it. Thus the reason why he preferred to work alone.

"Naturally," Ellen Pancrest went on, "my father wondered if he were the only one of his kind in the world. Was he unique— doomed to a lifetime of horrible loneliness? Or had Nature created others like him? The answer to these questions wasn't easy to determine, as the mutant characteristics were inner ones, and therefore not easy to identify. You could walk along a street, and one out of every ten persons you passed might be a mutant, but outwardly they would resemble anyone else. And there was the possibility that if one out of ten persons actually were mutants, they themselves might not be aware of it. My father himself didn't awake to the fact that he was radically different—a mutant—until rather late in life.

"But finally he hit upon a plan for learning whether or not there were others like him. That was when he abandoned inventing and started his Phrenarchy movement. The meaning of the word should be obvious enough; literally it means mind-rule, or rule of mind. Phrenarchy was a socio-political ideology, calling for an end to corruption, tyranny, and incompetence in government, with all their harmful and hindering effects upon society in general, by creating a government only of those who by their intelligence, character, and training were best fitted to govern. By a subtle emphasis upon intelligence and the clever use of highly advanced ideas and principles, my father made the concept one which psychologically would be of strong appeal to mutants like himself—if there were any.

"He found that there were a surprising number of them, in fact. Phrenarchy spread rapidly. Not all who joined were mutants, but these gradually were weeded out; and with the mutants who had first responded as a foundation, my father eventually built up the present organization of Neo-men, as he had come to call them."

DALL said abruptly, "But these other mutants—where in the world did they come from? According to my knowledge of the subject, mutations are caused by hard radiations like X-rays and Cosmic rays. But it's a haphazard process, similar to shooting at a distant, moving target while blindfolded. The chances are overwhelmingly against the occurrence of a good or beneficial mutation, and just about indefinitely against a beneficial mutation being duplicated."

Ellen Pancrest nodded. "True enough, if you consider that mutations are caused only by hard radiations working at random. But there are other influences that can cause mutations, Mr. Dall—and not at random, but deliberately."

"Deliberately," Dall muttered. He stared at the girl and said slowly, "You mean artificially...by machine?"

"Neither. There is one specific influence which you—and a great many others—have completely overlooked. Thought also can cause mutations. It has been proved that thought is a physical force, generated by the mysterious chemico-electrical functions of the brain. Thought, in fact, is the highest of the physical forces in that it recognizes no barriers of time, distance, or matter. Is it thus too far-fetched to suppose that thought itself might not be able to cause changes in the human germ plasma so as to bring about a mutation? I don't mean thought emanating from one individual, consciously directed, but thought emanating from individuals as a corporate mass, working subconsciously, in a sort of blind, instinctive urge for racial improvement.

"Man is subconsciously aware that he hasn't kept pace with the advances he has made in his environment. Subconsciously he feels his deficiencies keenly; subconsciously he is trying to overcome them. And such is the power of thought, such is its sheer, supernal intensity when produced by the collective mind of Man, that he can obtain just the changes in himself desired. That's how Neo-men came into being—not haphazardly or at random, but intentionally, through a kind of subconscious creation."

Ellen Pancrest paused, gazing quizzically at Dall. "Well, are you now satisfied about where the mutants—or Neo-men—came from?"

"Not so much satisfied as dizzy," Dall said.

The girl smiled slightly and resumed, "Once the Neo-men had been gathered and organized, realization came that they would sooner or later fall under the suspicions, and quite possibly the persecutions, of the Old Race. Phrenarchy already was being attacked as a subversive movement. The Neo-men couldn't hope to carry on their activities in secret; discovery would inevitably result. The only solution was to find a place where they could work indefinitely, without fear of eventually being detected. And the only place with exactly the right qualifications of remoteness was the Moon.

"The next thing my father did was to build a space rocket—a rocket, Mr. Dall, remarkably like your own. In this rocket, with two companions, he succeeded in reaching the Moon. And there, on the side eternally hidden from Earth, he found this city, which he named Lunapolis."

DALL said in surprise, "Then the Neo-men didn't build the city?"

"No, Mr. Dall."

"But who did?"

"We don't know. The city was here. As far as my father knew, it had always been here. It was deserted, completely devoid of life, but its buildings, together with their furnishings, utensils, and machines, were intact. These showed the builders of the city to have been a Huminoid race—and further, a race even more highly advanced mentally than Neo-men themselves. My father called this vanished people the Ultra-men. What had happened to them, why and how they disappeared, are things that we shall probably never know.

"What was most important to my father, however, was that the city was in perfect condition, just waiting for human occupancy. He decided to move the majority of Neo-men to Lunapolis, where they could follow their way of life in complete freedom from the hindrances of the Old Race.

"Much intensive research of the scientific devices in Lunapolis first was done. From this, among other things, came the drive principle of the degravity cruisers. A number of the craft were built in secret, and then Neo-men were ferried in from Earth. The cruisers were vastly more efficient than rockets, and made the exodus a thousand times safer and easy.

"All this, of course, took years. The constant grueling labor killed my father long before his time, but before he died, he had the satisfaction of seeing his work well under way. The Neo-men were in a place of ideal shelter and safety, organized under an ideal government; a government of those who, in intelligence, knowledge, character, and temperament, were perfectly suited for their tasks. My father had been the first Phrenarch; to me was given the honor of carrying on in his place."

"Which must mean," Dall said, "that you're completely a Neo-man—or Neo-woman, that is."

Ellen Pancrest nodded. "My father didn't marry until he found a mate among his own kind. This was shortly after he began his Phrenarchy movement. I was born on Earth, but have spent the last dozen years of my life in Lunapolis."

Abruptly the girl leaned forward, her green eyes intent on Dall's face. "Why do you think I've been telling you all this? Why do you think I've bothered with you to this extent at all?"

Dall shrugged. "Maybe it's because you like the way my eyelashes curl up. Or maybe you just felt like doing some talking."

"Hardly," Ellen Pancrest said. "I'm not in the habit of doing things on impulses; I try always to have serious and important reasons. In the present instance, my reason for having taken you into my confidence is based upon your outmaneuvering of General Melgard in the various phases of his activities against you back on Earth. You see, Mr. Dall, you, too, are a Neo-man."

CHAPTER THIRTEEN

UTTER surprise and incredulity jerked Dall to his feet. He burst out:

"What kind of a cheap trick—" He didn't finish; he fell silent abruptly as the irrefutable logic behind the girl's announcement dawned upon him. Melgard...outmaneuvered... That was it. He had been blind not to have realized sooner the implications of the feat.

The girl was watching Dall closely. She nodded a trifle, as though in grave satisfaction at what she saw.

"Exactly, Mr. Dall. Whatever else he may be, General Melgard is a Neo-man. Which means that he has an extraordinarily swift and keen mind, lightning-fast reflexes, and an unusual degree of physical strength. Yet you overcame him in hand-to-hand combat, shot down another Neo-man, and escaped from a degravity cruiser piloted by still another. How did you manage to do those things, when it's evident that no man of the Old Race is capable of defeating a Neo-man on equal terms? That's what you did, you know, despite the fact of an unknown, mysterious ally having revived you from the effects of the drug Melgard used. The only explanation for your success is that you also are a Neo-man."

Dall was silent, stunned. He recalled now the strange feeling that had come over him during the fight with Melgard; a feeling which, he had since dimly guessed, was the only reason for his triumph. And he recalled Frontenac's remark to the effect that he, Dall, possessed physical and mental qualities a great deal like those of the inhabitants of Lunapolis.

The truth of his new identity seemed inescapable—final and complete. But Dall knew it was something to which he'd be a long time in growing fully accustomed.

He glanced at Frontenac. The other was staring startledly at him, with a kind of uneasy wonder. Under his gaze Frontenac's dark eyes shifted quickly, evasively. An odd sensation almost like sickness struck Dall. Suddenly and shockingly, he realized that the revelation of his being a Neo-man had thrown a barrier between Frontenac and himself—a barrier that might be impossible to break down.

Ellen Pancrest, when Dall returned his attention to her, was lighting a cigarette. If she had noticed the little by-play, she gave no outward evidence of it. She met his look quietly, gestured toward the cigarette box and desk lighter in front of her, and said, "Have one?"

"Thanks." Dall selected and lighted a cigarette, and returned to his chair. He drew the smoke in deeply, striving to order the confusion in his mind. After a moment he abruptly became aware of what seemed an inconsistency. He said:

"Logic indicates that I'm a Neo-man—a mutant. But the facts upon which this conclusion is based are either misleading, or a paradox is somehow involved. To judge from what you told me about your father, mutants are rather easily recognized as different. And if my understanding is correct, Neo-men possess their mutant abilities all the time rather than just occasionally.

"Then how does it happen that neither I nor the people with whom I've associated ever guessed that I was fundamentally different? Why should the mutant abilities credited to me have appeared only during my encounters with Melgard and the others… Hartley and the cruiser pilot? Can it be that I'm just an ordinary man after all, but possessing somehow abilities that are supposed to be typical only of Neo-men?"

ELLEN PANCREST shook her head, smiling faintly. "It's simply because you are a Neo-man in whom the mutant characteristics are usually dormant, through a subtle variation in the basic mutation itself. This dormant quality is a clever protective mechanism, which makes possible a higher degree of survival value. Naturally, if a mutation is completely beneficial, it provides adaptations to all features and conditions of the environment, which includes protection from the obsolete but still dominant species that is a major and important part of that environment.

"It was relatively only a short time ago that Neo-man psychologists learned such a dormant quality of the mutation exists. Mutants possessing it are called Latents. It has been determined that there are a large number of Latents—true Neo-men who do not suspect, and who by their speech and actions give no cause to suspect that they are essentially different. Their superior abilities appear only in times of supreme crisis, such as when their lives or the lives of others close to them are threatened with immediate danger."

Dall was studying the burning tip of his cigarette, recalling once more the strange sensation he had felt during his fight with

Melgard. It had obviously lasted long enough to aid him against Hartley and the cruiser pilot, though in the stress of events he'd been aware of nothing unusual.

Slowly he realized that the girl was watching him, as if waiting for his reaction to her words. Her expression was assured, complacent. A dull, hopeless anger stirred within him. She had him trapped—and quite obviously she knew it. There was no way he could deny the things she had told him, and yet his very instinct revolted against admitting she might be right.

Ellen Pancrest said, "You hardly seem happy about the situation, Mr. Dall."

"Why should I be?" he demanded. "My experiences with Neo-men have convinced me they're anything but benefactors of humanity. To be one of them is far from what I consider an honor."

The girl's green eyes narrowed, her face hardened. "Just what do you mean by that?"

"For one thing, there's the sabotage that has been carried out by Neo-men against Earth's rocket research," Dall explained, with grim emphasis. "Quite a number of lives have been taken in this ruthless and horribly thorough campaign. A huge amount of scientific knowledge and progress has been lost, not to mention the waste in time, money, and human effort.

"And for what?" A note of weary savagery entered his voice. "For the lowest, most selfish reasons imaginable. Neo-men want to prevent the discovery of Lunapolis because of plans for a war against Earth. Melgard revealed as much in a little speech he made to the welcoming committee that met Frontenac and me when we landed here. War...simply and obviously because Neo-men consider themselves superior beings and therefore entitled to rule the roost. Probably the idea behind it is the old and idiotically altruistic one of making the world safe for...something; in this case, safe for Neo-men."

THE truculence had left Ellen Pancrest's face, but there was a determined set to her lips, and a cool defiance showed in her green eyes. She crushed out her cigarette with quick, decisive movements, then leaned forward, elbows resting on the desk, fingers interlocked. She said quietly:

"In some ways you're right, Mr. Dall. In others you're wrong...perhaps because you haven't taken certain facts into consideration. Neo-men do want to make the world safe for Neo-men. The idea may seem selfish—even despicable. But actually it's altruistic enough, and in no way that could be called idiotic.

"What you overlooked is that the evolutionary process that has acted upon the Old Race to produce Neo-men is still going on. It hasn't stopped. The Old Race is evolving. Eventually there will no longer be an Old Race, but a complete and homogeneous race of Neo-men. The Old Race is thus the seed from which will come the flower of the new race. For that reason it must be protected."

"Protected?" Dall snorted.

The girl nodded imperturbably. "Protected from itself. You know very well that the war back in the Forties was followed by dissension, bitterness, and deep distrust between nations, which formerly had been allies. It's no secret that a desperate and feverish atomic armaments race has since then been going on. Today the Old Race is prepared and poised for war—war with atomic weapons deadly enough to wipe out civilization.

"Nothing, as the situation on Earth now stands, can prevent that war. Each nation involved knows of the preparations that the others have made. This knowledge, together with endless and increasing political friction, has intensified enormously the original bitterness and distrust. And with the speed and destructiveness of atomic warfare, each nation knows its only hopes for supremacy, and even survival, lie in attacking first. Thus a state of unbearable nervous tension exists, in which even so much as a wrong word or look will precipitate the crisis."

She nodded at Dall. "You admit this much?"

"You've stated it pretty baldly," Dall said. "The various governments of Earth are at present loudly proclaiming undying faith and friendship for each other, but what you've said is essentially true. Earth is sitting on the biggest powder keg in civilized history."

"Exactly," Ellen Pancrest said. "And there you have the reason why Neo-men wish to prevent the discovery of Lunapolis—not because of any selfish motives of their own, but because the information might be the one, final thing needed to set off that powder keg. With matters on Earth as they are, the news of a city on the Moon would be taken to mean that some one government had secretly built the city as a base from which to launch its attack. And at once the atomic holocaust would begin.

"Mr. Dall, Neo-men are working to prevent that catastrophe. Since the Old Race is the seed from which will come the flower of the new, that seed must not be destroyed—even of itself. The new race must be given its chance to live. And it must be given its chance to nourish and grow. It must have tools and books, food and shelter…not the blasted ruins and dead, sterile ashes of destruction."

A FLAME seemed to kindle in the girl's face, and despite himself Dall felt an answering glow. She went on, her voice soft and intense.

"Earth is the heritage of the Neo-men. That heritage must be protected. Nothing will turn Earth's present masters from their path to utter ruin. Every appeal to reason, to the faintest instincts of kindness and decency, would be futile. The only solution is for some outside power to step in and take over by force the management of Earth's affairs. And Neo-men intend to do just that."

The glow faded from Dall. He shook his head slowly. "That doesn't alter the basic facts. It's still conquest."

"But conquest with permanent peace as its prime object, Mr. Dall, not conquest for power or gain. The Neo-men are waging what essentially is a peace war, and as their leader I've done everything possible to keep their activities in strict accordance with the conduct of such a war. If the object were power alone, you know, I could simply sit back and allow Earth to exhaust itself in its own struggles, and then with hardly any effort walk in and take control. I could even have permitted Lunapolis to be discovered, so as to hasten such an event. But I took the time, patience, and trouble of blocking Earth's rocket progress to prevent that; and I did it in a way that wouldn't reveal the presence of an outside power—knowledge which would have set things off as much as the discovery of Lunapolis itself. I had the rockets sabotaged while still on Earth…tampered with in such a manner that their destruction would be laid to weaknesses in rocket technology. If the rockets had been apprehended in space, their disappearances would have indicated the existence of an outside power, with the results already described.

"Furthermore, Mr. Dall, I've given my agents strict orders to avoid taking lives in carrying out their duties. I know that a number of men have died as a result of the rocket sabotage, but these deaths have been explained as unavoidable or accidental. I have recently learned, however, that many of them were due to mistakes or indifference. I intend to make a thorough investigation to find just where the blame lies. Those guilty of having disobeyed my orders will be demoted to positions where they will unable to cause harm in the future. General Melgard, I might mention, is one of them." She shrugged slightly and went on:

"The campaign against Earth's rocket progress is—or rather was—just a preliminary, but the actual war itself will also be fought as much without bloodshed as possible. Perhaps, Mr. Dall, you will insist that can't be done. Then let me hasten to point out that the preparations for this war have been years in the making. The plans were drafted by the owners of the finest minds in existence-Neo-men. And the weapons to be used are themselves like nothing ever known on Earth.

"I have already explained that examination of the scientific devices left behind by the former inhabitants of Lunapolis furnished Neo-men with the drive principle of the degravity cruisers. A large number of other discoveries were made. In many cases Neo-men were able to improve on what they learned, or to make radically new applications of their knowledge. Thus, as weapons for a bloodless peace war, Neo-men have the degravity cruisers, faster and more maneuverable than anything possessed by the Old Race; paralysis beams that will render the largest army helpless in a matter of minutes; fields, like the field enclosing Lunapolis itself, which within their zone of influence will make impossible the operation of internal combustion engines and prevent the firing of rockets or artillery; and finally, Mr. Dall, force shields, which will dampen the explosions of atomic bombs and absorb their deadly radiations.

"And, remember, the users of these weapons will be Neo-men, the finest soldiers and technicians in existence; men far above average in intelligence and training, with unusually keen minds, steel nerves, and enormously swift reactions. If this alone weren't enough—" Ellen Pancrest broke off, smiling at Dall with a curious mixture of mockery and triumph. She said softly:

"Mr. Dall, where would a highly intelligent and clever people like the Neo-men be if not in government positions of high authority?" A momentary grimness touched her smile. "And that's just where they are. Those already in key positions either joined the Neo-men ranks or aided others to obtain equally important posts. Today Neo-men hold key positions in every government of every nation on Earth. They are in essence a fifth-column organization the like of which has never been equaled. At a signal they are ready to go into action. When that signal comes, the organization of every country on Earth will be thrown into confusion and utter chaos—and the Neo-man armies will quietly and efficiently step in to take over. The whole affair will be finished before anyone completely realizes what has happened."

ELLEN PANCREST'S voice went into silence. The smile went with it, leaving her fine features grave and faintly quizzical. Her green eyes searched Dall's face.

Dall was only dimly aware of it. He was staring woodenly at the floor. He had a baffled, helpless feeling; somewhat the feeling of a man who, setting his nets for minnows, has caught a whale. He saw everything now, and it was big—much bigger than he had ever even remotely guessed it might be. This city on the Moon had foundations so deep that they were rooted in the entire social and political structure of Earth itself.

Frontenac was gazing steadily and motionlessly through the huge window in the wall beyond the desk. Bitterness lay in the curve of his lips, and his dark eyes were shadowed and sad.

After a moment the girl said, "Mr. Dall, I've explained all this to you not merely because you're a Neo-man, but also in the hope that the information would influence you into joining the Neo-man organization. New additions are always welcome. If you agree to join, you will be given rank and duties equal to your abilities as determined by intelligence, aptitude, and psychological tests."

"And if I refuse?" Dall suggested.

"If you refuse, you will be put to work as a prisoner of a status equal to that of a prisoner of war. You will be without freedom, without such advantages as leisure, better food and living quarters, and social intercourse.

"But there is no reason for you to refuse. Neo-men are fighting for peace. And with their organization, abilities, and weapons, they can't lose. Neo-men will prevent the impending worldwide atomic war. They will prevent all war. They will unite Earth under one government—a government of those who, as shown by objective, unprejudiced scientific tests, are in every way most perfectly fitted for their duties. And Neo-men will abolish tyranny, crime, famine, and corruption. They will improve living conditions, increase the general level of knowledge, health, and prosperity. They will, in short, work to bring on a true Golden Age."

Ellen Pancrest gestured. "I won't try to hurry you, Mr. Dall. The fact that you're a Latent complicates matters, since you require a longer period of assimilation, rationalization, and adjustment. But if you aren't a complete fool, you'll realize eventually that you won't be making a mistake in joining. I'll give you enough time to think it over. For the present, that will be all."

She touched one of a number of buttons set in the surface of her desk. A moment later the double doors at the rear of the room swung open, and a squad of guards filed in.

Ellen Pancrest indicated Dall and Frontenac with a casual wave of one slim hand. Her face was cool and indifferent, her green eyes remote. She said:

"Return these men to their apartment. The guard over them will be maintained until further notice."

Dall rose as the guards came forward. He glanced at the girl, and for an instant her eyes met his. Something flashed from them in that brief meeting, something that seemed secretly pleading and anxious. And for some odd, indefinable reason it struck into the very nucleus of his being.

Then the guards were gripping his arms, and in a turmoil of emotions he was led away.

HE REMEMBERED little of the elevator ride that followed, and the bleakly silent walk through the halls. Only when he and Frontenac were once more alone in their room did full awareness of his surroundings return.

Frontenac smiled with a perceptible effort. "Well, Harvey, it's been an interesting morning—or whatever you call it here, on the Moon."

"I wouldn't say so." Dall was uncomfortably aware of the forced quality of Frontenac's smile. Too vivid recollection came of the strange, new unease and evasiveness that had come over Frontenac after Ellen Pancrest's strange revelation that Dall was a Neo-man. The change from the old, easy and comradely state of relations was one that filled Dall with hurt and uncertainty.

"Why not?" Frontenac demanded, a note of false heartiness in his tone. "Interesting is the only way to describe it. We were in a tough spot for a while…prisoners in the enemy camp and all that. Then it turns out that friend Harvey is some sort of a little tin god, and the keys of the city are promptly extended on a golden platter."

Dall managed a grin. "Tin god? You mean this Neo-man business. It could still be a trick, you know, in spite of everything."

Frontenac shook his dark head gravely. "I don't believe that, Harvey, and I know you don't either. All the various facts Ellen Pancrest brought out fit in just a bit too well for that."

"Maybe. But if I'm actually a Neo-man, then being a Latent as well hardly makes me a tin god."

"It brought you an invitation to join the fold," Frontenac pointed out. "So it must be important." He paused. He said too casually, "I suppose you'll join?"

Dall was silent for some moments. "I may have to," he said at last. "If only as a trick. You know what I am, Jules; you know the oath I took. I can't go back on that. As a prisoner I'd be useless, but as a member of the organization I'd be able to get around and learn things. It's possible that eventually I'd be able to find a way for us to escape—or even to upset the Neo-man applecart."

Frontenac looked sardonic. "Why beat around the bush, Harvey? This thing's too big to upset. And even if we did manage to escape, the news of a city on the Moon might very well start trouble. But if by some miracle it doesn't, what could be done about the Neo-men and their plans? The nations of Earth have no way of reaching Lunapolis after what's been done to rocket research. And the Neo-men would clamp down immediately at any attempt to purge them from Earth's governments.

"Any way you look at it, Harvey, the Neo-men are certain to come out on top. The oath you took isn't important when you consider that. It's an oath involving something that literally doesn't exist anymore. So I can't exactly blame you for wanting to join; it's wise to get in on the winning side while the getting in is good. Only don't try to spare my feelings at being left out. I don't count. I'm just a common, ordinary human being. When Ellen Pancrest remembers I exist, I'll be given some sort of slave labor and will be out of your way. Then you can enjoy—"

Dall grasped Frontenac's shoulders, his fingers biting deep. "Jules—do I really deserve all that?" Anguish twisted his face and thickened his voice.

Frontenac took a deep, unsteady breath. "No…I guess you don't. I…I'm sorry. Everything just sort of got me. It's the end in a way, you know—the end of all I'd thought was good and normal and permanent. I haven't got over it yet."

DALL turned away. Amid a thick, strained silence, he crossed the room and lowered himself heavily into a chair. Frontenac was right, he realized. It was the end of the old order of things. There seemed nothing he could do about it. The political situation on Earth was too explosive to risk disturbing with the information he possessed—even if he could manage to escape with it first. And the Neo-man organization was too big an applecart for one man alone to upset.

Suddenly he wondered if he actually did want to do something about it. If Ellen Pancrest hadn't lied, if Neo-men could bring peace, freedom, prosperity, and enlightenment, it might be a good thing after all for Neo-men to take over the management of Earth's affairs. There could be no doubt but that Earth badly needed unified capable leadership in the terrible crisis it faced.

And there was the new race dawning; a better, stronger race. Who could deny that it should not have every opportunity for a place in the sun?

A better race…Dall thought abruptly of Melgard, recalling his experiences with the man. Melgard was cruel, ruthless, utterly without mercy or compunction. For all his vaunted Neo-man superiority of intelligence and nervous reactions, he still had all the innate animal savagery of the Old Race. Perhaps intensified and increased, as all the other Neo-man qualities seemed to be. And Melgard would hardly be an exception. There would be others like him—many of them.

Dismay and misgivings surged through Dall. Ellen Pancrest dreamed and planned and looked forward into a golden future. She was altruistic, an idealist. But how many of the other Neo-men also shared her dreams and ideals? If Melgard was an example, and the officers who had shown such interest in his traitorous plans, was the Neo-man organization actually rotten to the core—filled with power-hungry, potential tyrants, who would enslave and exploit rather than enlighten and uplift?

Dall remembered his oath. He saw that huge room once more, with its dusty, old-fashioned furniture and the grim-faced men, armed with machine guns, spaced on guard around the walls. He heard Merrick's voice again, and his own voice responding. *"I do solemnly swear..."* Words that bound him; words that had become a part of him. He couldn't go back on them.

Somehow, he told himself, there ought to be a solution to all these conflicting elements. Somehow there ought to be a way out. He had to find it. He clenched his big-boned hands tightly, and the lines deepened in his angular, brown face. *He had to find it!*

There was a knock at the door. A moment later a guard carrying a tray entered the room. A number of things instantly caught Dall's attention. The guard was in a strange hurry; excitement showed in his face. Two others, visible in the hall, stood in attitudes of unmistakable tension, drawn weapons held in their hands. And through the opened doorway came a hubbub of sound: the shouting of voices mingled chaotically with the pounding of feet.

"What is it?" Dall demanded. "What's happening?"

"That," the guard said, depositing his burden, "is what we intend to find out." He ran from the room, and the door slammed shut.

Ignoring the tray, Dall crossed to the panel and placed his ear against a seam, listening intently. As far as he could make out, the mysterious uproar was continuing. He listened for a long time. At last there was silence.

Frowning, with a vague feeling of anxiety, he turned away. What could possibly have taken place?

"Harvey Dall."

A whisper of something that was not sound. Over it, emphasizing it, came a sharp, shocked exhalation that could only have issued from Frontenac.

Dall's eye jerked up. Framed in the bedroom doorway he saw—

The white-haired man!

CHAPTER FOURTEEN

NOTHING about the mysterious and rather incredible stranger appeared to have changed. The conservative dark suit he wore seemed to be the same in which Dall had last seen him. The thick mane of snow-white hair was the same, as were the intense dark eyes below, and the pale, smooth, ascetic face.

Looking at the other, Dall had an odd sense of disorientation. It was for all the world as if he were back on Earth instead on the Moon, in a hidden, fantastic city, and the stranger had stepped from another room, with all the ease and casualness of one who had been there all the time. And the stranger's appearance in no way destroyed the illusion; he looked neat, calm, and completely unruffled, as though that supernally cold, empty, and airless gulf between the Earth and its satellite were no more than a short walk along a well-paved path.

The incongruity of it struck Dall with numbing force. Momentarily he looked past the other and into the bedroom. He was certain the room had utterly no means of entrance. There was only one door, and this opening into a closet.

The closet! That was it! For the first time, Dall noticed that the closet door hung open. By craning his neck, he could see part of an opening in the closet—an opening that could have been made only by a hidden panel.

He swung his glance back to the stranger, questions erupting volcano-like in his mind. Words leaped to his lips, but as he met the penetrating, hypnotic eyes, something unseen and intangible, yet with all the power and materiality of a hand, came to choke off speech. Once again, as on that day in the forest, he felt helpless, frozen; felt as though his mind was being searched— read as one reads the pages of a book.

Then full awareness of himself and his surroundings returned. He had a vague feeling of outrage, as of one whose personal privacy has been disturbed—not rudely, perhaps, but nevertheless invaded. He said slowly:

"I don't think I care for that little trick you seem to have."

"I am deeply sorry," came the silent mental response. "I would not have done so were it not unavoidably necessary."

AFTER a moment Dall shrugged. "All right, it was necessary. But how did you manage to reach the Moon? How did you get into this room?"

"The city has many secrets, and these are known to me. As to how I reached the Moon, let it be sufficient that I have done so. There is no time for explanations of this sort."

"You ought to be able to tell me a few things," Dall persisted. "I need something to go on. And—say, how did you find out where Frontenac and I were being kept? How did you know the exact building, the exact room?"

"Your own thoughts led me to you. My knowledge of the city accomplished the rest. My name...let it be Jonothan. Actually it is a purely mental pattern or configuration that would be meaningless to you. It is not important; Jonothan will suffice. And as to who I am—or more accurately, when considering the implications behind your question, what I am— the term Ultra-man will be sufficiently if partially illuminating."

Jonothan moved one slim hand in a gesture. It was as if the movement had torn aside a curtain or opened a concealing door, for Dall had a sudden, vivid impression of deep anxiety, a burning inner tension.

"Now you must heed without interruptions what I have to say," Jonothan went on in his weirdly silent manner. "Disastrous events are occurring within the city. A new and terrible danger threatens not only Earth, but Neo-men as well. And, I had better add, you also, Harvey Dall.

"This danger has arisen from the very midst of the Neo-men themselves. The mutation that produced them, you see, was not a completely beneficial one, for while Neo-men have improved brains and nervous systems, they still possess certain basic flaws of human nature inherent in what has been termed the Old Race. The most prominent are hereditary criminal tendencies that, if not properly diverted by training and environment, cause much harm and loss to society. Neo-men inherited these tendencies—but greatly increased and heightened, just as their superior abilities are an increase and heightening of abilities possessed by the Old Race. The increase and heightening of these tendencies within Neo-men, however, has given them such a powerful hold that neither training nor environment has the slightest dampening or ameliorating effect. Criminal Neo-men are therefore enormously more cunning, vicious, and destructive than their Old Race counterparts.

"A group of such criminal Neo-men has instigated a rebellion within the city...Lunapolis...with the object of seizing control of the entire Neo-man organization. It is vitally important that they be prevented from carrying out their plans. Because of a certain factor, which I shall presently explain, they have excellent chances of winning Lunapolis; but once the uprising is extended to Earth, they will meet with constant opposition from the majority of the fifth-column forces stationed there, and a conflict will result will involve both Neo-men and the Old Race. Even if the rebels do succeed in the end, it will be to set up in the ruins of Earth a rule of such tyranny, suppression, and violence that civilization may never again recover.

"But that is only the first consideration. For, if the rebels are defeated, the Neo-man organization as a whole must in turn be prevented from carrying out its plans. It is the nature of the Old Race that it refuses to be led, except when it has itself selected its leaders. A despotic rule by Neo-men, however benevolent and progressive it might be, is doomed to failure. All the history of Earth has shown that nothing won by force is ever permanent. Only when achieved by peaceful co-operation can there be unity."

An impulsive protest leaped to Dall's lips. "But the impending atomic war on Earth—"

"Would automatically be prevented if Neo-men peacefully joined forces with the Old Race," Jonathan finished. "For Neo-men possess certain scientific knowledge that would render atomic warfare harmless—if not actually impossible."

DALL spread his hands helplessly.

"I don't see why you've told me all this. There's nothing I could do to stop the rebels—or the Neo-man organization, for that matter. What about Ellen Pancrest? Doesn't she know about the rebels?"

"She soon will—but it may be too late. Warning her will avail nothing in the long run, since she also must be defeated. I have mentioned that there is a certain factor that gives the rebels excellent chances of success. This factor is the Control."

"The…Control?"

"I will explain. Lunapolis, you see, is a mutant city. In effect it is an entity, for its operation and functions are coordinated, centralized, and guided in a way that produces a kind of independent, pseudo-sentient existence. A fair description of the city might be made with respect to the human body itself. Some machines act as heart, lungs, nerves, and limbs. Forces generated by others act as bloodstream and mental and nervous impulses. There are also devices that act as sensory organs.

"The Control is the brain of the city. It superintends and regulates the manufacture, generation, and distribution of power, light, heat, artificial gravity, air, water, and even food. Thus any individual or group in possession of the Control is literally in possession of the city as well. And of the other persons within it—for the city is filled with various powerful forces, held in leash, and operated beneficially. These forces, however, are potentially deadly and destructive when the activities of the Control are interfered with by human operation. The Control was so designed as to respond to human thought, such as would be necessary in an emergency. An individual in possession of it can therefore direct the deadly force of the city against other individuals. This is a fatal flaw that the builders of the city were unable to foresee, primarily because they did not envision tenants other than themselves.

"Ellen Pancrest is now in possession of the Control. It is the plan of the rebels to strike by surprise and deprive her of it. By that one single act they hope to become the masters of Luna-polis.

"Harvey Dall, you are wondering what all this has to do with you. You know that possession of the Control will prevent the rebels from carrying out their uprising. You know that possession of the Control will destroy the Neo-man organization; for the Neo-men in Lunapolis are the guiding force of that organization, and with the city and its occupants dominated by a hostile party, the Neo-men will be helpless—paralyzed.

"You, Harvey Dall, know the issues at stake. You must obtain possession of the Control for me, since I can most easily and efficiently take advantage of its powers. I have a duty, too, you see.

"The Control is kept in a special chamber, here, in Capitol Tower. I know secret ways of the city, and can lead you to it with little risk."

"But why can't you get at it yourself?" Dall demanded in perplexity. "Why do you have to use me as an agent?"

Jonothan's answering thoughts were sad and faintly bitter.

"Simply because I am psychologically unable to perform directly any action that would result in harm or injury to a living creature. I am so constituted mentally that the merest thought of it is painful and revolting. Thus I must use you as a proxy. Naturally, once you enter the chamber of the Control, you will meet with immediate and deadly resistance. This resistance will have to be overcome in…drastic ways."

"How do I know I can trust you?" Dall questioned abruptly. "How do I know this isn't some kind of an involved and clever trick?"

"You know I can be trusted, Harvey Dall. You have only to look into my mind."

"…Yes—I can see."

"And you will do it?"

FOR some queer reason Dall hesitated. He knew what so clearly and inescapably was his duty; he knew the only answer he could make. But Ellen Pancrest's face was suddenly vivid in his mind—not the cold and arrogant face, but the gentle and lovely one. He saw her green eyes, soft and shining, dreaming of a better future. Then he saw her defeated, humbled, her dreams shattered into dust—and something ached within him that he had never felt before.

And then he saw the picture Jonothan had painted; saw it in every sordid and ugly detail. Nothing of dreams, this, but stern and hideous reality. He glanced slowly at the plain platinum watch strapped to his wrist. The scales were more than balanced the other way…

He nodded. "I'll do it."

"Then we will start at once," Jonothan said, with swift purpose. "Not a moment can be—" The thought broke; Jonothan stiffened, his intense dark eyes flashing toward the door. His soundless mental voice gasped in Dall's mind.

"Danger! A group of Neo-men coming…fast—so fast!" And then Jonothan whirled and was leaping toward the hidden opening in the closet.

Even as he moved, the door to the apartment burst open with a crash, and three uniformed Neo-men, gripping rifles, catapulted inside. Dall stared dazedly at the figure in the lead. Recognition came with a wrenching shock.

Melgard! Melgard—who by now should have been far off in space, well on his way back to Earth!

For an instant Melgard paused, his hard, burning eyes sweeping the room. His glance touched Dall and Frontenac—darted to the bedroom doorway. In a flash of motion he reached it. He saw Jonothan.

Jonothan was half inside the secret closet opening. His attention was drawn by Melgard's abrupt appearance—and for the tiniest moment he hesitated.

With a man of Melgard's lightning reactions, it was disastrous. Melgard whipped up his rifle, pressed the trigger.

Dall, standing on a line with the bedroom doorway and the closet beyond, saw in all its frightful details the thing that happened. He saw the rifle whip up, heard its dull, coughing chatter, saw the continuous, almost solid stream of tiny tungsten-steel shells that poured forth. He saw Jonothan fall back into the opening; his face and head dissolving in bloody ruin. Then the hidden panel slid shut, and the nightmare horror of the scene was mercifully gone.

Split-seconds of blurred speed and Jonothan was—dead!

CHAPTER FIFTEEN

HARDLY had the secret opening closed, when Melgard again was in motion. He hurried into the closet and ran his hands over the edges of the obstructing panel, as though seeking some concealed lever or switch. He found nothing, for he pounded the panel irritably with the flat of one hand. Finally he picked up his rifle. He hit the panel several times with the end of the stock, listening intently. Then, with a shrug, he returned to the living room.

"Metal," he told the two Neo-men, who had accompanied him into the apartment. "Would take a cutting torch to get through, and there's no time for that. The spy—or whatever he was—is dead, anyway."

Feet pounded in the hall, and a new group of uniformed Neo-men appeared in the open doorway. The officer in command took a few steps into the room, saluting as his glance fell on Melgard.

"Need any help, General?"

"All in control, here," Melgard grunted. "Continue mopping up, Lieutenant."

"Very well, sir!" The officer saluted again and whirled back into the hall. His voice lifted in sharp command; then came the pounding of feet once more, this time fading away.

Dall was rigid, his big hands clenched against the sick despair inside him. Dead! Jonothan was dead! The only person with the knowledge and abilities capable of defeating the Neo-men was gone. And the very thing Jonothan had warned against apparently had happened; the criminal element of Lunapolis—of which Melgard seemed the leader—evidently had their uprising well under way. Utter catastrophe was in the making—and Dall was helpless.

He thought suddenly of Ellen Pancrest. Was she safe? Or had she been taken prisoner…possibly killed? The speculation was oddly dismaying. He tried to tell himself that the girl meant nothing to him, that he didn't care what happened to her—but failed.

In another moment Dall became aware that Melgard was watching him. The rebel commander's blunt features wore a thin smile of triumph. Mockery glinted in his eyes, but their blue depths showed other emotions as well. Hate was there, and a sadistic eagerness held carefully in check. It seemed obvious that Melgard was relishing the opportunity to exact full payment for his defeat at Dall's hands in the fight back on Earth.

"Well, Dall, here we go again," Melgard said at last.

Dall nodded gravely. "Then hang on, General—so you won't get left behind as usual."

The muscles around Melgard's square mouth grew pale. The mockery faded from his eyes, leaving the vindictive hatred beneath to glare nakedly. He spoke in a voice that had thickened.

"You won't get away from me this time. I'd have had you when you first landed here, if the Phrenarch hadn't stepped in. But she won't be able to help you anymore, so if you're smart you'll skip, the wisecracks. I'm not saying it'll make things any easier for you, but you'll live a little longer."

"What happened to Ellen Pancrest?" Dall demanded. "What have you done with her?"

MELGARD'S lips curled in a jeer. "Such tender concern… The Phrenarch gets them all that way—even on short notice. She hasn't been hurt, if that's what you're worried about. She's being held prisoner in her apartment. When I wind up this business, I'll see that she doesn't get lonesome." The jeer broadened.

For an instant Dall had a wild urge to leap forward in complete disregard of the rifles held watchfully by Melgard's two companions. He remained motionless. It took an effort that brought beads of perspiration to his forehead. He said quietly:

"I thought you were on the way back to Earth. Ellen Pancrest said you had left."

"That's exactly the impression I wanted to give. I only pretended to leave. The ship took off without me. I picked the crew from my own men, so the Phrenarch and her boy scouts wouldn't find out. You see, Dall, I guessed the reason why the Phrenarch had ordered me back to Earth. I didn't intend to give her any time to set a trap for me." Melgard seemed eager for an opportunity to boast.

Dall nodded. "One more thing. How did you know there was someone here, in the apartment, with Frontenac and me?"

"These rooms are specially reserved for the Phrenarch's enemies. Which means they have something other rooms don't—hidden microphones. When my men started taking over Capitol Tower, I detailed one of them to listen in on you. Later he came running to tell me something funny was going on. I was near this floor, and decided to look in... Good thing I did."

Melgard's hard blue eyes narrowed searchingly. "Who was that man, Dall? What was he doing here? I already know he was a spy of some sort. He was seen sneaking around Lunapolis a few times, but we couldn't catch him."

"He wanted me to help him get something he called the Control," Dall said. He shrugged in pretended indifference. "I didn't trust him. I tried to get him to tell me who he was and what he was up to, but he just said there wasn't time to explain anything. That's about all."

Melgard looked doubtful. His eyes continued their search. Finally he shrugged and said, "He wouldn't have got anywhere with the idea he had. My men have the Control under guard. They had a stiff fight getting it, and anybody who wants to take it away from them will have to put up an even stiffer fight... The Control's atomic stuff, in case you don't know it, Dall.

When the news got out that I had captured it, resistance stopped all over Lunapolis. I didn't even have to put on a demonstration."

"Too bad," Dall said. "I'll bet you were disappointed."

Melgard moved so fast that he hardly seemed to move at all. The barrel of his rifle thudded viciously against the side of Dall's head.

A burst of light, a roar of pain; Dall staggered back, stumbled against a chair, and fell to the floor. He lay still for a long moment, fighting the nausea and the whirling blackness that sought to overwhelm him. The room finally steadied. Agony throbbed like a pair of huge, overworked lungs in his head, but he found that he could think through it. And he could move. He climbed slowly back to his feet.

"You cracked wise once too often," Melgard said. "Think twice before you do it again."

Dall said softly, "Put up your gun, General. Send your bodyguards out of the room. For five minutes. That's all I ask—just five minutes."

MELGARD moved his free hand in a sharp gesture. A mask seemed to have dropped over his face. "Sorry, Dall, I've a lot of work waiting for me. And I've already wasted enough time on you." He turned to the two Neo-men nearby. "Major Rankin, Captain Boyd, I want you personally to take these men down to the Council Chamber and see that they are placed under guard with the other prisoners. Take no risks with them. At any slightest sign of resistance, shoot to kill."

Rankin and Boyd nodded grimly and saluted. With a last vengeful glare at Dall, Melgard turned and stalked from the room.

"All right, you two," Rankin said. "Let's start moving."

Dall glanced hopelessly at Frontenac. The smaller man didn't seem to notice. His dark eyes had a set, glazed look. The march of events, bewildering in their swiftness and complexity, appeared to have dazed him. Dall felt a leaden surprise that his own mind was able to stand up under the strain.

Boyd shoved Frontenac toward the door, and at a prod from the point of Rankin's rifle, Dall followed. They were marched through the halls, to the elevators. Faint noises of activity sounded throughout the building. There were distant screams, mingling with shouted commands and the thumping of feet. Occasionally a rifle chattered.

Rankin emitted a short, sarcastic laugh. "Those dumb civilians," he told Boyd. "They know what capture of the Control means, but they still try to hold out."

"It's all over, though," Boyd responded. "And they know it. They're just taking things the hard way."

There was a small crowd of captives under guard before the elevator doors. They were composed both of civilians and soldiers, obviously loyal to Ellen Pancrest.

The elevators were being used far over capacity; it was a long while before a car finally stopped at their floor. Rankin immediately commandeered it, and Dall and Frontenac were ordered inside.

As the car descended, Dall looked at Rankin and said mildly, "Melgard seems to be a big noise up here."

"Why not?" Rankin demanded. "He was commanding general of the Neo-man army before the uprising. He got the job because he had a higher int-apt rating than any other officer."

Dall echoed, "Int-apt?"

"Intelligence and aptitude," Rankin explained. "As decided by tests. That's the system here, you know."

"Yeah. But why did the Phrenarch use a man as important as that against small change like me?"

"She claimed an officer with the highest abilities was needed in your case. General Melgard was the natural choice. His opinion of the matter is that she was afraid of him, and wanted him out of the way."

"And your opinion?"

"She didn't like or trust—" Rankin stiffened and his face went carefully blank. "Don't ask for my opinions," he snapped.

Boyd was frowning at Dall. He asked abruptly, "How did it happen that you tripped up the General back on Earth?"

DALL shrugged. "Nothing much to it. He doped me, but I was able to throw it off. Then he had a gun on me. I jumped him, knocked him out, and tied him up. He managed to escape, though, and made for a degravity cruiser hidden a short distance away. I followed in a flitterjet. He tried to ram me with the cruiser, but I dodged out of the way and pulled a trick that made him think I was dead."

Rankin brought the elevator to a sudden stop between floors. "You're not trying to pull a fast one?"

"I wouldn't be here if Melgard was everything he's cracked up to be," Dall answered quietly.

Boyd said, "If you did all that, it can only mean—"

Dall nodded. "I know. I'm a Neo-man."

"And not only that," Rankin said slowly. "For you to have licked General Melgard also means…" His voice trailed off. He glanced with cryptic significance at Boyd. Then, in unison, the two turned their heads to look at Dall. Their faces showed varying degrees of something that seemed a mixture of awe and respect.

Dall said, "What got you men to join Melgard in his plan to double-cross the Phrenarch?"

"He promised us important posts on Earth," Rankin answered. "After it was conquered, of course. If the Phrenarch had her way, the Neo-man army would be just a bunch of nursemaids for the Old Race."

"Important posts," Dall snorted in derision. "There won't be any important posts if Melgard has *his* way—or anything else, for that matter. Hasn't it occurred to you that everything depends on the fifth-column forces on Earth? Suppose the fifth-column refuses to join Melgard when it learns what has happened here? He'd have three strikes against him right from the start.

"And don't overlook the fact that a war of conquest demands all of the striking power that's available. It's a safe guess that less than half the Neo-men in Lunapolis are on Melgard's side. What could he hope to accomplish with that many?

"Even if half the fifth-column forces joined Melgard, the other half would immediately start all kinds of trouble. It would push the Old Race into war in an attempt to catch Melgard and his collaborators in between. With only half an army, he simply wouldn't have time to do anything. Earth would be laid waste in a matter of days. There aren't any important posts in a world of radioactive ruins, mutated vegetation and rotting corpses."

Dall's voice became low and vehement. "Don't you think Melgard doesn't know that? Of course he does! I'll tell you what he's up to. He's trying to spoil absolutely everything. He had failed on an important mission. He had disobeyed certain orders. He was slated for demotion—possibly outright removal. And he certainly knew it. He's a poor loser. He's the sort who, when dragged down, tries to drag everyone else down with him."

Rankin and Boyd looked at each other again. They said nothing. Deep and perturbed thought showed on their faces.

A signal light glowed on the elevator control panel. Those awaiting use of the car, obviously were growing impatient.

"Melgard must be stopped," Dall stated, with quiet intensity. "It might not be too late. If I had the right kind of men to help me—"

"General Melgard has the Control," Rankin pointed out. "You wouldn't be able to do anything."

"But maybe the Phrenarch would," Dall persisted. "If she were to be rescued, she might know a way out of the mess."

The signal light went on again. Rankin gestured irritably and said, "If you're trying to talk me into something, Dall, you're wasting your breath." Features hardening stonily, he put the car back into motion.

Dall slumped in leaden despair. A nice try, he thought bitterly. Too bad it had been wasted.

CHAPTER SIXTEEN

THE car descended only a few floors more before Rankin brought it to a stop again. Dall and Frontenac were prodded out into a great hall. Captive Neo-men of both sexes filled the hall in a long, moving line. They were being herded through a huge doorway at the end. The elevators constantly disgorged new additions to the parade. Rebel guards, clutching their rifles in grim alertness, were strung out at close intervals along the walls. Despite the numbers of those present, there was a heavy, ominous silence, broken only by the shuffle of feet, the soft sibilance of the elevators, and an occasional harsh command.

After a short study of the scene, Rankin and Boyd obtained the assistance of a rebel soldier. With the latter running interference, Dall and Frontenac were taken down one side the procession of captives, toward the doorway at the hall's end.

The doorway gave into a vast chamber, filled with semi-circular rows of tiered seats, which sloped down to an officiating rostrum at the opposite end. Rebel officers of the Neo-man army, obviously high-ranking, were seated behind the rostrum, engaged in activities that Dall could not immediately decipher. The entering captives, he noticed, were roughly being herded into seats by groups of armed soldiers. Other soldiers, placed at numerous points about the chamber, were on guard behind mounted machine weapons.

Dall and Frontenac were now marched down the steps of an aisle, toward the rostrum. They were brought to a halt several paces away, while Rankin and Boyd stepped forward. The two saluted crisply, and Rankin proceeded to explain why Dall and Frontenac were there.

Glancing over the faces of the officers, Dall saw among them the four who had been with Melgard when the *Frontier* landed in Lunapolis. They were listening gravely. Dall thought they looked tired. And somehow they gave a faint yet persistent impression of unease, as though their complicity in the uprising were something they had begun to regret.

Rankin appeared to notice it, too. Even while he spoke his eyes moved quickly and intently over the faces of the four. Then, evidently to conceal his reactions, his features became carefully blank.

When Rankin finished, he and Boyd saluted again and left. As they went, Dall saw them exchange a swift glance—a glance, it seemed, of mutual understanding. He wondered what it meant. It had seemed to mean something, but he knew it could just as well have meant nothing at all. Rankin and Boyd were the sort of team who would always glance at each other.

THE officers conferred briefly, studying Dall with obvious interest. Then a detail of soldiers was summoned, and Dall and Frontenac were placed under guard in seats a short distance to one side of the rostrum.

With dispirited interest, Dall watched the activities that were going on. One by one the captives present were being brought before the rostrum. Their names were taken, along with their occupations and rank. It appeared that they were persons important in the administrative, military, and scientific circles of Lunapolis. With a lie detector carefully checking their responses, they were questioned about the nature of their resistance to the rebels, which had resulted in their being taken captive. Then they were carefully quizzed in regard to the degree of cooperation that the rebels could expect in the future. Some were dismissed as a result of the questioning. Others were led out by soldiers, to be kept in detention. And there were those sent to a certain heavily guarded section of seats at one side of the chamber. They were the doomed. Dall felt a chill, realizing that a remorseless and thorough purge was taking place.

He glanced at Frontenac, who sat slumped dejectedly in the seat beside him. The other returned his look with a wry smile.

"The same old story, eh, Harvey?" he murmured. "The victors and the vanquished—even among a people like the Neomen; even in a city on the Moon."

"Yeah." Dall scowled his disgust. "To think that one single thing like the Control gives a skunk like Melgard the power to do this! If Jonothan had only managed to get away..." Dall glanced inquiringly at Frontenac. "Is this over your head? Or did the white-haired man tune you in on his telepathic broadcast?"

Frontenac nodded. "It was the strangest experience I've ever had. Like hearing a voice that somehow made no sound at all."

"Jonothan could read thoughts as well," Dall said. "If he hadn't been concentrating so heavily on us, he might have detected Melgard sooner and had more time to get away. Jonothan was the only hope we had—and he's dead."

"So this really is it, eh?" Frontenac chuckled mirthlessly. "And I was worried about a nice, safe, comfy little thing like being put to work..."

"What Melgard plans to do with us is going to make work a pleasure by comparison."

"But isn't there something we can do? There ought to be something, Harvey—no matter how hare-brained and useless. We can't just go out like...*like sheep*."

Dall glanced significantly at the grimly alert guards who ringed them about, just out of earshot. "Not right away, anyhow. But we'll do something, Jules. A chance will come. If I can use what's inside me—if I can move fast enough to get at Melgard..."

Dall smiled, a quiet, sad, and terrible smile.

FRONTENAC was silent a long moment. Then he reached out abruptly and touched Dall's arm. "Whatever happens,

Harvey, I want you to know I'm sorry for the way I acted a while ago."

"I've already forgotten it, Jules."

"But I haven't. You see, Harvey, my sense of perspectives got twisted. You worked for me; from a financial viewpoint, I was your superior. But it was a difference of degree rather than kind. It didn't make you any less human than I. It didn't make you any less a friend. Learning that you were a Neo-man made me lose sight of these things. It made you different…superior. Then it came to me that this, too, was only a difference of degree rather than kind. You were still human; still a friend.

"And I guess the same goes for Neo-men and the Old Race in general. The difference between them is only one of degree. Neo-men are still human—what's happening here right now proves that. If they were to get their perspectives unkinked, they'd see that friendship with the Old Race was entirely possible. And the Old Race could be made to see it the same way, where Neo-men are concerned. What each needs is simply a chance to get together."

Dall shook his head somberly. "Melgard isn't going to give them that chance."

"Yes," Frontenac said. "Melgard."

Preoccupied silence fell once more. Dall returned his attention to the proceedings in the Council Chamber. He noticed that the influx of captives had dwindled to a mere trickle and finally ceased altogether. There weren't as many of these as he had first thought there would be. The captives were mostly persons important in the affairs of Lunapolis, and as anywhere else they constituted only a small part of the total population. The tribunal of rebel officers was rapidly whittling down the numbers of those who remained.

Dall glanced toward the section of seats where, kept under heavy guard, sat the Neo-men whom the tribunal had condemned to death. Their ranks had steadily grown. At least one had been added for every person dismissed or kept prisoner.

The rebel inquisition—or this initial phase of it—finally drew to a close. Melgard had been busy directing various other details of the uprising from his headquarters in another part of the building. The officers in the Council Chamber, however, had been in almost constant communication with him by visiphone. Acting now on instructions received from Melgard, they ordered the doomed captives taken outside, to the landing field near Capitol Tower. Immediate execution was the reason clearly implied.

The orders included Dall and Frontenac also. Under the watchful eyes of their guards, they were herded outside with the others.

Dall found that Lunapolis hadn't as yet been lowered once more within its concealing crater shaft, for the landing field was bathed in sunlight. The city was still in the Sunset zone of the Moon's eternally hidden side; and would be for a considerable time longer, since the Lunar day was fifteen Earth days in duration.

With the others, Dall was marched to the approximate center of the landing field. Orders were given to halt, and the guards took up positions on all sides, their rifles leveled in silent warning.

Dall watched bleakly. It soon became evident that he and his fellow prisoners were not to be executed by rifle fire. The guards seemed to be waiting for something, merely maintaining watch. Just what, he wondered, was Melgard planning to do?

WITHIN minutes came the sound of approaching feet. A group of rebel officers strode briskly into view. In the fore of the procession was Melgard, holding in his hands a square crystal case the size of a man's head. As he came nearer, Dall saw that the case was transparent, for within it he could discern an infinitely complex mass of tubes, wires, and metal parts. The mechanism seemed, in some obscure way, to be in motion, for innumerable tiny colored lights glowed, pulsed, and shifted within it.

A realization burst within Dall. The object Melgard carried could be only one thing—the Control!

Melgard came to a stop several paces away. He surveyed the assembled captives slowly, a thin, sardonic smile twisting his square lips. Momentarily his eyes rested on Dall and Frontenac, and the smile broadened, grew mockingly triumphant. Then his eyes passed on; a harshly purposeful expression appeared on his face. He said:

"You people are all outspoken enemies of the new administration. Since most of you hold important posts in Lunapolis, no chances can be taken that you might eventually try to use your influence and knowledge against us. It would serve no useful purpose to keep you prisoners indefinitely. Your refusals to co-operate can thus mean only one thing—death."

"Death is preferable to co-operation with a pack of traitors and military criminals," returned a gray-haired, erect man in uniform, who stood near Dall. He added, "And I'm sure that I speak for my fellow prisoners as well."

There were quick murmurs of assent.

Melgard moved his heavy shoulders in a shrug, smiling in grim amusement. "Considering the fact that you are all going to die anyway, I'll overlook your lack of respect. It'll make up for the traditional hearty meal that the condemned are supposed to be fed. As to how you're going to die…" Melgard held out the crystal case. "This is the Control. As you no doubt know, it operates the powerful and deadly forces that fill Lunapolis. And it responds to human thought—which means that anyone who has it can also operate those forces.

"What I'm going to do should be obvious. I'm going to order the Control to blast all of you out of existence. The execution will be over in an instant. There won't be any pain; no fuss, no waste—nothing. Nice, isn't it?" Melgard rocked back on his heels, grinning. "You're going to have a few minutes to think about how nice it is. I've ordered the Phrenarch brought here, so she wouldn't miss out on the fun. Until she arrives, just relax and enjoy yourselves."

Dall said, "You're walking into a trap, Melgard. I wouldn't bother to warn you if it weren't for the fact that you're not the only one in Lunapolis who would get hurt."

Melgard stiffened, his blunt features puzzled and suspicious. "Just what do you mean?"

"The Control holds the various forces of the city in a highly delicate balance," Dall responded. "Interfering with its operation destroys that balance. Lunapolis will blow apart like an atomic bomb."

Melgard shook his head in disbelief, but his eyes were intent, perceptibly worried. "You're lying, Dall. You're just trying to pull a trick to gain time."

Dall shrugged. "All right, I'm lying. But when Lunapolis blows up, just remember I warned you."

THERE was a deep silence. Melgard bit his lip, frowning. Behind him, his rebel cohorts were whispering in apprehensive speculation.

Melgard said finally, "It has to be a trick, Dall. You're a stranger here. You don't know anything about the Control, or how it works."

"Don't forget the spy you shot in my room," Dall said. "He wasn't a stranger here. He knew all about the Control—and for that matter, he knew more about it than you and the others can ever hope to know. He told me a few things; enough to know what I'm talking about right now."

Melgard's frown deepened. A baffled uncertainty verging on anger showed in his eyes.

In the tense quiet that ensued came the sound of footsteps. Two soldiers approached the group of rebel officers, striding swiftly from the direction of Capitol Tower.

Melgard turned to glance at the arrivals. His face dilated in alarmed surprise. "Where's the Phrenarch?" he demanded. "I thought I told you to bring her here."

"There must be some sort of a mistake, General Melgard," one of the soldiers answered. "The Phrenarch wasn't in her apartment. The guards on duty there told us that you had already sent Major Rankin and Captain Boyd after her."

Melgard said with deadly flatness, "I didn't send Major Rankin and Captain Boyd after the Phrenarch. If they said I sent them, it can only mean they're pulling a double-cross. But why should they—"

Abruptly Melgard whirled back to Dall. "You're the one who put them up to it," he snarled. "I ordered Rankin and Boyd to take you to the Council Chamber. That gave you the chance to fill them with a lot of smooth lies. You were worried about the Phrenarch. You fixed it so that Rankin and Boyd would sneak her away somewhere."

Dall shook his head. "This is as much of a surprise to me as it is to you."

"More lies," Melgard spat. His features were drawn and pale with fury. "Rankin and Boyd wouldn't have tried anything like that alone. The only explanation is that someone put them up to it. And you're the one who did it, *Dall*. You lied to them in some way—just as you lied to me about the Control."

Melgard grew icily calm. "The Phrenarch can't hope to get away. With the Control, I'll locate her in a matter of minutes. That goes for Rankin and Boyd, too. As for you, Dall, you're going to pay for your meddling—right now!" With a swift, implacably deliberate movement, Melgard raised the Control. He peered into it, staring in concentration.

In the bare instant of life that he knew remained to him, Dall could only watch in frozen despair. His story about the danger involving use of the Control had been a pretense. He had realized that Melgard's authority was vested almost solely in the Control, and he had hoped to undermine that authority to the extent where an attack upon Melgard could be made. Neo-men were...*fast!* An attack upon Melgard could succeed only if grave doubts about his prestige existed in the minds of his followers. These doubts would slow the otherwise lightning-quick Neo-man reactions, giving Dall the time he needed. He hadn't been certain that he could move fast enough to get at Melgard before the watching rebel soldiers cut him down.

But his efforts had been destroyed by the news that Rankin and Boyd had freed Ellen Pancrest. There would be no further chance to attack. Even now Melgard was hurling his mental commands at the Control. In another moment death would strike.

CHAPTER SEVENTEEN

IN ANOTHER moment…Melgard was hammering his thoughts at the Control. Its crystal case glittered in his hands. Its internal mechanism glowed and shifted.

A moment passed. Another. Seconds passed. And then minutes.

Nothing happened.

Sweat shone on Melgard's forehead. Sweat glistened in beads on his upper lip. He stared into the Control, straining in furious concentration.

Still nothing happened.

Striking into the tight-drawn silence came a peal of silvery laughter, mocking, triumphant.

With an explosive gasp, Melgard whirled. Utter consternation twisted his face at what he saw.

Hardly a dozen yards away stood Ellen Pancrest. With her were Rankin and Boyd. Obviously, with the attention of everyone focused on Melgard and Dall, the trio had been able to approach unnoticed.

Gazing at Ellen Pancrest, Dall's eyes widened in sudden discovery. In her hands she held a square crystal case identical to Melgard's. No, he amended an instant later; not quite identical. For the tiny colored lights within the one held by the girl were brighter, moving with more intense activity. And somehow the crystal case seemed to exude an almost tangible aura of power.

Green eyes sharp and intent, Ellen Pancrest was glancing warily from Melgard to the rebel minions about him. Her features were stern and coldly determined. She spoke in quiet warning.

"Don't any of you move. What I have here is the real Control—not a clever imitation like General Melgard's. I don't have to tell you what I can do if you try to disobey me."

Melgard growled, "So I was tricked."

Ellen Pancrest inclined her gold-glinting brown head in a grave nod. "I suspected you for quite some time, General. That's why I kept you busy on Earth. I knew, however, that I couldn't keep it up indefinitely, and that sooner or later you would try to take matters into your own hands. Thus I took the precaution of having an imitation of the Control made in secret and substituted for the real one. Since the Control can function wherever in Lunapolis it might be, it was in no way handicapped by removal from its normal resting place."

"I see..." Melgard threw a withering look at Rankin and Boyd. *"Traitors,"* he snapped. "If I could only get my hands on you..."

Rankin and Boyd glanced at each other. They grinned in total unconcern.

Evidently angered by their defiance, Melgard swung his gaze furiously to the girl. "Major Rankin and Captain Boyd are dangerously untrustworthy. You've seen how easily they switch their loyalties. If you're wise you'll have them executed as traitors immediately."

Ellen Pancrest smiled slightly and shrugged. "Like all intelligent persons, Major Rankin and Captain Boyd are opportunists. They adapt themselves to prevailing conditions. Regardless of what they might have done, they have redeemed themselves to my complete satisfaction." She straightened purposefully, her green eyes moving over the rebel assemblage. "Now—lay down your weapons. And let me warn you against trying to be clever."

THE warning proved to be wasted. Ellen Pancrest had momentarily taken her eyes off Melgard—which was a serious mistake.

Melgard had been holding the fake Control. Now, with a smooth flashing motion, he hurled it at the girl.

She saw it coming. Evidently realizing that there would be no time to use the Control, she ducked.

During the split-second while she was forced on the defensive, Melgard's hand darted to the gun holstered at his side. He jerked it loose, whipped it up, aimed it. At the same time his finger was tightening on the trigger.

Dall had been dazed by the bewilderingly rapid shifting of events. But the threat of immediate and deadly danger to Ellen Pancrest jolted him into instant awareness. It was as though an electric current had shot through him.

And—again something happened. Again he experienced that uncanny feeling of vibrant, surging strength. Again his mind was oddly sharp and clear, registering the details of his surroundings with a fire-bright, crystalline vividness.

Even as Melgard aimed the gun, Dall hurled himself forward in a leap at the other's legs. The gun blasted as Melgard went down, the bullet smashing harmlessly skyward. Then Melgard hit the ground, with Dall sprawling atop him.

Though shaken by the impact, Melgard reacted with frantic speed. He chopped down with his gun hand, bringing the muzzle of the weapon into line with Dall's back. Dall, however, was moving. He had flipped himself over in a roll toward Melgard's gun arm. His shoulder struck the weapon aside just as Melgard squeezed the trigger, and once more the shot went wild.

In a continuation of his original movement, Dall caught Melgard's wrist in both hands and tumbled clear. He began working instantly and with savage haste to tear loose the weapon clutched in Melgard's imprisoned hand. Desperately, doggedly, Melgard maintained his grip. Even in this crisis he didn't lose his presence of mind. Instead of pulling against Dall, he threw himself forward and with his free hand began raining in punches to Dall's head.

Keeping his double grip on Melgard's wrist, Dall threshed and writhed out of range. Melgard flung himself in pursuit with a violent heave of his body. He came down partially atop Dall, and now his free hand darted out and fastened on Dall's throat. Eagerly and with furious strength, he began to squeeze, his fingers constricting as inexorably as the jaws of a closing vise.

Pinned down, forced to retain his hold on Melgard's gun hand to prevent the weapon from being brought into play, Dall was at a disadvantage. Slowly, as his breath was cut off, the world began to cloud and grow dim.

It was no time for the niceties of combat. Pouring his last dregs of strength into one final supreme effort, Dall twisted from under Melgard. For a moment they were locked chest to chest. In that moment Dall made his last bid for victory. He brought his knee crashing into Melgard's groin.

A number of things happened in rapid succession.

Melgard had been pulling against Dall with his gun arm. Now he stiffened under a spasm of pain. At the same time his finger tightened involuntarily on the trigger of the gun. The weapon was an automatic type, which fired as long as the trigger was depressed and the ammunition supply lasted. Agony kept Melgard's finger on the trigger, though active fighting strength had momentarily left him.

TO DALL it was unexpected—and almost disastrous. He, too, had been pulling. No longer meeting with resistance, he found the spitting weapon jerked abruptly toward him. Bullets ripped through the flesh of his left arm and shoulder. With frantic haste, impelled more by pain than logical thought, he twisted the muzzle aside. Simultaneously he pushed. Melgard's finger was still locked spastically on the trigger. The lethal stream caught him full in the face. Under the supreme on-slaught of death he stiffened again. And then, his features unspeakably shattered and crimsoned, he went limp in lifelessness.

It was a moment before Dall completely realized what had happened. He was dazed and incredulous at the suddenness of the battle's end. Finally he stood up, becoming conscious as he did so of the excruciating burn and throb in his injured arm and shoulder. A red stream was pulsing from the wounds, dripping from the tips of his fingers.

He became aware of sounds, the exultant shouting of voices. He glanced up to see men running toward him. He recognized them in an oddly distant way. Frontenac was in the lead. After him came Rankin and Boyd.

He saw all this through a thickening haze. The scene whirled chaotically and grew dark. He felt hands touch him, and then a deep soft blackness came to engulf all further thought and sensation.

Dall walked down the long dark corridor toward the light shining at its end. The corridor grew curiously shorter as he moved, as though contracting of itself. Suddenly he was in the light. It touched him with a strange insistence. For the first time he realized that his eyes were closed. He opened them.

Light again, reflected softly from the walls of a room. He blinked, puzzled by vague yet disturbing memories.

There was a thin whisper of sound. His eyes caught a flicker of movement. Turning his head, he saw a face. A face with cool green eyes and red lips, framed in gold-glinting brown hair.

The face of Ellen Pancrest.

She smiled and said, "I was beginning to think you'd never awake."

Dall digested her words slowly. The disturbing memories took solid form. Realization that he had been unconscious came to him with a feeling of surprise.

"So I passed out, eh? I must be getting old, if a little scrap can do that to me."

"I'd hardly call it a little scrap," Ellen Pancrest said. "Melgard choked you half unconscious, and then you had at least a dozen bullets pumped into you. That, I should think, is enough to make anyone pass out."

"I won't argue the point." Dall glanced curiously about him. He found, as he had already sensed, that he was lying in a bed. The room was unfamiliar; it was larger than the room he had shared with Frontenac, more luxuriously furnished.

He looked inquiringly at the girl, who sat in a chair at the side of the bed. "Where am I?"

"I had you moved to another part of Capitol Tower. As a convenience due to your having been wounded."

"I see." Reminded of his injuries, Dall glanced at the bandages swathing the upper half of his left arm and most of the shoulder. He moved the arm experimentally and was rewarded by a stab of pain.

"You shouldn't do that," Ellen Pancrest admonished. "You must remain quiet as much as possible. The best surgeons in Lunapolis treated you, and they claim they did an excellent job—but you'll have to co-operate, you know."

DALL grinned wryly. "It hurts not to co-operate, so I guess I'll have to." He sobered. "Considering that I've been bandaged up instead of executed, I'd say you have things in order again."

"Very much in order," the girl returned. "With Melgard dead and the Control in my hands, the rebels promptly decided that discretion was the better part of valor. The bad characters among them have been weeded out, and are being given certain psychological treatments, which will render them incapable of making trouble in the future. As for the others, they merely went along with the tide, so to speak, and are harmless under ordinary circumstances. Lunapolis is almost back to normal— thanks to you, Harvey Dall; you made it possible. By placing serious doubts about Melgard in the minds of Rankin and Boyd, you indirectly accomplished my rescue and this gave me the opportunity to reach the place where I had hidden the real Control. I had been unable to do so previously, since I actually thought Melgard had left for Earth, with the result that the uprising took me completely by surprise. And as if the rescue alone weren't enough, Harvey Dall, you further saved the day when you prevented Melgard from killing me."

Dall moved his good shoulder in a shrug. "Think nothing of it. I often get the urge to play boy scout."

"Perhaps. I, however, consider your help too important to take lightly, involving as it did the fate of all loyal Neo-men and of the Old Race as well—not to mention my own life. I'd like somehow to show my appreciation."

"You would? Then suppose you permit Frontenac and me to return to Earth?"

Hurt and disappointment leaped into Ellen Pancrest's strong, fine-carved features. She glanced away, shaking her head. "I…I couldn't do that."

Dall said gravely, "It would seem that your appreciation doesn't run very deep."

She stiffened as though struck. "No—you mustn't think that! Consider, Harvey Dall. You know the situation on Earth; you know what the knowledge of Lunapolis and the Neo-men would do. I couldn't take the risk that you might release this knowledge—with, of course, the humane if mistaken idea that unpleasant results could somehow be avoided."

"Suppose I promised not to reveal what I know? Would you show your appreciation on this basis, by permitting Frontenac and me to return?"

"I think I would, Harvey Dall—but only where your promise alone is concerned."

"You mean you wouldn't accept a promise made by Frontenac?"

"He isn't a Neo-man. His promise would mean nothing."

"That puts me right back where I started from," Dall said slowly. "Frontenac is my friend. He and I are in this together. I wouldn't consider leaving him behind."

Ellen Pancrest moved her slim hands in an abrupt gesture. "You've overlooked what is actually the most important issue, Harvey Dall. The question isn't so much whether you should be permitted to return to Earth—and Frontenac with you—but whether there is any logical reason why you should wish to return at all."

"The simple desire to return is logical enough, the way I see it," Dall said.

"But you're a Neo-man!" she pointed out with emphatic swiftness. "Your place is here, with others of your kind. To be quite frank, we need new additions like you, Harvey Dall. And Lunapolis offers opportunities that you'd never find on Earth. It would be more than worth your while to join the Neo-man organization."

Dall grinned crookedly. "It's your way or nothing, isn't that it? And you said you wanted to show me your appreciation for having been a good little boy scout."

THE girl's face twisted. She leaned toward the bed in sudden pleading. "Circumstances leave me no other alternative. You must believe that. The plans of the Neo-men are paramount to everything else. Nothing must endanger them—not even debts of gratitude." She hesitated a moment, green eyes fixed earnestly on Dall's face. Then she stood up. "You haven't had time to think the situation over thoroughly as yet. And the fact that you've been wounded further complicates matters. Considering this, it wouldn't be wise for either of us to jump to conclusions.

"And now I had better leave, I've kept you talking far too long. You really should be resting, you know." She smiled wanly, turned, and strode quickly from the room.

Dall gazed after her, his feelings oddly confused. He heard a murmur of voices from the room beyond, issuing from the door that the girl had opened in leaving. Moments later two persons entered the room. One was Frontenac, the other a stern-featured, elderly woman in white, clearly a nurse.

A wide grin on his thin, dark face, Frontenac gripped Dall's hand. "Ah, the hero of Lunapolis! Well, well! To ask the usual trite question, how do you feel?"

"Thoroughly punctured and deflated," Dall returned.

Further conversation was momentarily forestalled as the nurse efficiently bustled over Dall in a routine check over. Finally, recording her findings on a chart, she prepared to leave. She paused to glance disapprovingly at Frontenac.

"Remember," she said. "Ten minutes." She went out, closing the door behind her.

Frontenac grimaced and dropped into the chair beside the bed. "Ellen Pancrest and the nurse wouldn't let me in at first, but I argued them into letting me have ten minutes."

"If you can argue Ellen Pancrest into anything, you're a better man than I am," Dall said.

Frontenac's dark eyes narrowed shrewdly. "Why? Were you trying to do that?"

"Sort of." Dall reported the main points of his conversation with the girl. "Not that I expected her to let us go," he finished. "But she brought up the subject of her appreciation, and I thought I'd see what there was to it."

"So we're still prisoners, eh?" Frontenac said.

DALL nodded solemnly. "Even if we agree to toe the line, the fact that she intends to keep us away from Earth won't make much of a difference. Gold-plated chains, if you get what I mean. She claims that what we know about Lunapolis and the Neo-men would start trouble on Earth. I think there's another explanation. The political situation on Earth is bad—admitted. But evidently it isn't too bad. Otherwise she'd have little fear about permitting us to return. We'd keep our mouths shut rather than cause a worse mess than the Neo-men would make. What worries her is the possibility that, used in the right way, our knowledge would serve to unite Earth against the Neo-men instead of plunging it into war."

"There may be another reason, Harvey."

"What do you mean?"

"The lady may want to keep you here for—well, let's say purely personal interests. She's been with you off and on ever since you were wounded. Heroes deserve some pampering, I know, but there's a limit to everything. I don't think I'd be wrong in guessing that she has a crush on you."

Dall stared at the other in startled disbelief. Slowly the expression faded, to be replaced by one of deep thought. He smiled bleakly.

"If you're right, Jules, that may give us an opening. We've got to stop the Neo-men from carrying out their plans. And for best results it will have to be done at this end. Getting back to Earth with what we know is only a minor part of the job. This is war in a way. Anything goes—even to playing on Ellen Pancrest's girlish susceptibilities for the chance we need."

"I don't exactly see how using her would help us, Harvey."

"Lunapolis is the heart of the Neo-man organization," Dall explained. "We've already seen demonstrated the fact that the Control is potentially a gun pointed at that heart. And Ellen Pancrest is the shortest, most direct way of getting at the Control. If I could get hold of it by working through her, I could seriously cripple the preparations that have been going on here for the conquest of Earth. And then we could use the Control as a weapon to make an escape. We could even destroy all ships except the one we needed, so there would be no possibility that we might be followed or shot down."

Frontenac caught Dall's uninjured shoulder in a tense, eager grip. "It could be done, Harvey! It's the one thing that might work!"

"It'll mean joining the Neo-man organization," Dall added. "That's the quickest way of gaining Ellen Pancrest's confidence. And then, if she really has taken a fancy to old Casanova Dall, we're just as good as on our way back to Earth."

Frontenac's face clouded. He hesitated, then said slowly, "Are you really sure you'll be able to go through with it, Harvey?

You're a Neo-man, you know. And Ellen Pancrest is a mighty attractive girl."

Dall's metal-gray eyes were grim and steady. "If it can be done at all, Jules, you can be perfectly certain that I'll do it."

CHAPTER EIGHTEEN

UNDER the constant care of Neo-man physicians, Dall's recovery was rapid. Therapeutic devices of an advanced type were used, which greatly hastened the healing of his wounds.

Frontenac's surmise about Ellen Pancrest's interest in Dall seemed to be giving increasingly firmer basis in fact, for the girl was a frequent visitor. She made no further requests for Dall to join the Neo-men, obviously having decided that he should have ample time in which to consider his decision. And Dall, carefully playing his part, created no suspicion by bringing up the subject himself.

Despite his secret intentions, Dall gradually found that he looked forward to the girl's visits with feelings that verged dangerously on eagerness. He told himself it was due merely to the time-heavy monotony of his convalescence, but he couldn't deny that she was pleasant to look at as well as fascinating to talk to. She possessed an astonishingly wide range of knowledge, and her penetration of scientific matters, regardless of how technical and abstruse, often required a real effort on Dall's part to keep up with her. She could be serious and erudite or vivacious and amusing. Only when she spoke of the plans of the Neo-men did her talk take on a depressing note.

Among other things, Dall early discovered that Ellen Pancrest's air of coldness and dominating arrogance was only a pretense. Her true personality was essentially one of sympathy and warmth. As she herself explained in a moment of confiding:

"It isn't easy for a woman to manage an organization composed mostly of men. To get things done requires that one seem as little like a woman as possible. I know I have a reputation for being all claws and ice, but it's the only way to command respect and obedience."

The time came when Dall's arm and shoulder were finally released from their long confinement in bandages. By way of celebrating the event, Ellen Pancrest sent him an invitation to dinner. With it came a superbly tailored evening suit of dark blue synthe-wool, which had somehow been cut to his exact measurements.

Frontenac watched in bright-eyed interest as Dall dressed. "I think this is it, Harvey. She may pop the question tonight."

"I hope so," Dall answered. "I'm tired of beating around the bush. The sooner we go into action the better I'll like it." He wondered suddenly how much of his words were true. Was he actually anxious to destroy Ellen Pancrest's plans and return to Earth—quite possibly never to see her again? He told himself he was. It took an effort.

DALL and the girl ate alone, in an elegantly furnished room lighted only by candles. The setting was one suited more for romance than for intrigue involving the fate of a world. And Ellen Pancrest's appearance heightened the effect. She wore a simple yet exquisitely designed evening gown of some dull, dark green material that set off her eyes and contrasted startlingly with the creamy whiteness of her skin. Her gold-brown hair was upswept and covered with a mantilla-like, filmy jeweled net that fell in soft folds about her shoulders. An emerald necklace glittered at her throat, and there were matching emerald pendants at her ears.

Dall, who hitherto had seen her dressed mainly in severe, masculine-styled garments, found it difficult to think of her as the Phrenarch of Lunapolis. She was just Ellen Pancrest, as feminine and sweet as any simple, unspoiled girl of Earth. Her dazzling loveliness caught at him in a way that was oddly disturbing.

She seemed more than usually vivacious, but there were moments during the meal when Dall found her gazing at him in an intent, speculative way. It made him wary and tense. Suppose all this was nothing more than camouflage? Suppose the girl was putting on a clever act in an attempt to trap him? He whipped his mind to its highest pitch of alertness, determined to be prepared for whatever might happen.

Deliberately he threw himself into conversation, responding to the girl's sallies with all the wit and sparkle he could summon. If she were putting on an act, he intended to meet it with one that was fully as good.

Dinner over, Ellen Pancrest led the way to a luxurious sitting room. Before a huge, purely ornamental fireplace was an enormous semi-circular couch. Coffee and cigarettes were set out on a low round table within convenient reach. She poured coffee, indicated the cigarettes, and asked:

"Care to see a canned television program?"

"Canned?" Dall echoed uncertainly.

"A recording," the girl explained. "It's the only sort of television contact we have with Earth at present. Neo-man technicians, however, are working on apparatus with which they hope to span the gulf that separates us here, on the Moon."

"I'd certainly like to see a program—recording or anything else," Dall said. "I've almost forgotten there was such a thing as television."

The girl smiled. She went to the fireplace and touched what seemed a number of decorative projections. The lights dimmed; a large square mirror over the fireplace slid aside into the wall, revealing a screen. In a moment more, under her manipulations, the screen woke to vivid, full-colored life. Music flooded the room as a gay and clever operetta began to unfold.

Ellen Pancrest seated herself on the couch beside Dall and lighted a cigarette. She sipped her coffee and watched the screen, glancing at him occasionally as some particularly amusing situation occurred. He grinned back at her, outwardly casual and at ease, but inwardly disturbed at her nearness. He fought the feeling. He reminded himself that the girl could never mean anything to him. She was an enemy, and he was sworn to defeat her.

THE operetta drew to a close. Ellen Pancrest manipulated the fireplace controls again. The screen vanished behind its concealing mirror, and the sitting room lights came on.

"Like it?" she asked.

"A lot," Dall said. He grinned abruptly and added, "I guess I'm still a kid in some ways."

"I suppose we all are." She fell silent, studying her hands. Then, abruptly, she looked at Dall. "But we are grown up after all, you know. And as grown-ups frequently do, we have to make decisions. I've been patient with you, Harvey Dall— remarkably patient, in fact. But I think the time has come to ask if you've made your decision about joining the Neo-men."

Dall hesitated. As though to cover up his hesitation, he lighted a cigarette and rose. He went to stand before the fireplace, looking into it, as though somehow it held the answer he had to make. His back was to the girl, but he knew she would be watching him intently, waiting. Finally he turned.

"I knew you'd ask me to join sooner or later. I'd made up my mind to refuse—mainly because it seemed the only honorable thing to do. Earth has been home to me. The fact that I'm a Neo-man seemed to mean little by comparison."

He paused. He had been speaking slowly, gazing reflectively into space. Now he met Ellen Pancrest's green eyes. This was the most difficult part of his act. Everything depended on making the girl believe him. It would have to be good. He went on:

"That is, the fact meant little until just a short time ago. My experiences with the Neo-men have hardly been what might be called pleasant. They seemed a cold and ruthless lot. But I've since found that they're very much like people I've always known. Some are...very likeable. And...well, things have happened lately that make me glad I'm a Neo-man. I didn't want to admit it…pure stubbornness, I suppose. But now seems a time to face the facts."

"Then you'll join?" the girl said eagerly.

Dall nodded. "I'll join."

She was suddenly radiant. It was as though a light had leaped into being within her, illumining her face. She rose and went to stand before him. Her slim fingers touched his arm. She said simply:

"I'm glad…Harvey."

Looking into her shining eyes, Dall knew that he had won. He felt no triumph at the knowledge. His only sensation was one of deep and burning guilt.

An abrupt thought moved like a cloud behind Ellen Pancrest's green eyes; her radiance faded. She said slowly, "I'm not a complete fool, Harvey. Your acceptance could be a trick, you know. Suppose—just suppose I were to give you an examination by lie detector?"

Dismay clutched at Dall. Already having experienced the efficacy of the Neo-man device, he knew it would all too easily betray him. Even as the dismay came, however, he strained fiercely, frantically, to keep it from showing in his face. He met the searching green gaze and twisted his lips into just the right degree of hurt bitterness.

"So that's the way it is, eh?" His tone was deliberately flat, dead. "OK—bring on your lie detector. It won't tell anything you don't already know. But when it's over, I want you to remember something; I want you to remember that I'm through—completely. In fact, I have a good mind to call everything off right now."

"No! No, Harvey!" Her hands caught at him. Alarm showed in her face. And then came swift confusion. Her hands dropped; she looked away, biting her lip.

"I'm…I'm sorry, Harvey. I guess it's only natural to doubt where you want most to believe."

DALL looked at her. He said nothing. He couldn't trust himself to speak. His emotions were bright sword blades that flashed in conflict.

There was a brittle silence.

Ellen Pancrest turned, her features anxious and contrite. "I made an apology, Harvey. You haven't told me if it was accepted."

"Duly accepted," Dall said, his tone equable. "My folks worked hard to make a gentleman out of me, and I'd hate to disappoint them at a time like this."

The green eyes brightened. "I'll arrange for your tests first thing the next day-period. These will determine the exact place in the organization for which you're best fitted. And then, Harvey, you'll be given your first opportunity really to become acquainted with the Neo-men. You won't regret your decision, I assure you."

The tests proved extremely difficult. They instilled within Dall a deep respect for those Neo-men able to pass them with satisfactory grades. That these fortunates amply deserved the posts that they were given afterward, he had no doubt.

He concentrated desperately on his answers, but he despaired of ever winning a place among the Neo-men higher than that of an assistant mechanic. Thus his stupefaction was complete when Ellen Pancrest later informed him that he had come through with flying colors.

"The intelligence tests," she explained, "place you well above the Neo-man average. Taking into consideration the fact that you're a latent, this means a good deal. As for aptitude, ability, and all the rest, the tests show that you have exceptional skill as an engineer in practically all branches. Your particular knack, however, seems to lie in research work.

"Accordingly, you have been assigned to the experimental laboratories of the Engineering Corps, with the rank of captain. Later, if your record merits it, you will be given further tests. With added experience and training, it's possible that you'll be able to advance to a position as a special project supervisor, with the rank of lieutenant colonel or better. Since the Neo-man organization is a going concern, you will, of course, receive a salary. I might mention that the rate of pay is far higher than that which could be obtained in a corresponding post on Earth."

She hesitated. A small-girl shyness seemed to replace the crisp, businesslike manner which she had assumed for the moment.

"I'm having a small dinner party in my apartment this evening. I shall be happy to have you attend, if you wish. It will give you the opportunity to meet a few of the more important Neo-men in Lunapolis."

Dall grinned. "I'll be there with bells on—or the equivalent."

She grinned back, eagerly. "It's a date, then!"

CHAPTER NINETEEN

MORE dinner parties followed. Quite often—and they were occasions to which, Dall realized guiltily, he looked forward with particular excitement—he and Ellen Pancrest ate alone. They spoke animatedly and exhaustively of the myriad topics in which they shared a mutual interest. Their discussions took place with little or no regard for time, frequently lasting far into the night. They began to interrupt, then to contradict each other. And then they began to argue. Their arguments, for some reason, however, always ended in a draw.

There were other evenings when they drove in swift, bullet-like degravity cars through the broad, futuristic avenues of Lunapolis, or strolled along the network of aerial spans, oblivious to the dizzying gulfs beneath them. And once, in ponderous metal suits, they ventured out upon the desolate, airless surface of the Moon.

Lunapolis was temporarily in the sunrise zone of the side eternally hidden from Earth, a time especially suitable for a jaunt, since surface conditions were roughly on a borderline between the inferno-like heat of the Lunar day and the utter, near-spacial cold of the Lunar night. Dall and Ellen—for it was by her first name that he thought of her and addressed her now—were not alone; a group of guides, all seasoned veterans of exploring trips over the wild and tumultuous landscape, accompanied them.

This particular trip almost ended in tragedy, for as he and Ellen descended the steep slope of a large crater, an outthrust bit of hardened lava upon which Dall had precariously balanced himself gave brittlely under his weight. Amid swift-settling clouds of ash-like pumice he went rolling end over end down the slope, to the crater floor, moving with grotesque slowness in the Moon's lesser gravity. It was this that saved him, together with the cushioning effect of the pumice drifts and the stoutness of his electronically heated air-suit.

Dall was dazed and shaken, but unhurt. He barely had time to realize what had happened when Ellen appeared beside him, her face bloodless and her green eyes dilated with fear. Despite the guides, she had been the first to reach him. Only later did he become aware of the incredible risks that she had taken in the effort to get here.

Fumblingly, frantically, she sought to lift his head. Her voice sounded in his helmet earphones, shrill with a concern that she made no attempt to hide.

"Harvey! Harvey—answer me! Have you been hurt?"

"I'm...I'm all right, I guess." Dall grinned feebly at the girl. Then, as her intense anxiety registered upon him, he stared. He hadn't guessed that she was capable of such solicitude on his part. It made thought of the task before him all the more unpleasant.

Under his intent, startled gaze, her long lashes dropped. She was oddly subdued for the remainder of the trip, which, at Dall's own insistence, was resumed.

Ellen later vetoed further trips beyond Lunapolis. As a substitute, she took Dall on sightseeing tours through the city's vast factories and laboratories. He was at once awed and dismayed by the myriad, complex forms of industry that met his eyes. Through his own line of work he had gained an idea of the scope of Neo-man activities, but he hadn't guessed that these were actually so extensive. In the factories enormous, robot-like machines turned out a seemingly limitless variety of products, while in the laboratories experiments in all fields of research—including some that Dall hadn't known existed—constantly improved old products and brought to light new ones.

DALL was surprised to learn that a large number of the articles being developed and manufactured were of a type employed for peaceful purposes. And the fact that these were being turned out in huge quantities caused him considerable perplexity. He had supposed that the Neo-men would be engaged chiefly in the all-out production of war materials, considering their plans for the conquest of Earth.

"The manufacture of war equipment is naturally an important part of the Neo-man program," Ellen explained, when Dall had put his puzzlement into words. "But it can hardly be called the most important part. Neo-men must have money—and money running into millions of dollars—with which to purchase on Earth the wide variety of supplies, raw materials, and other items that either are lacking on the Moon, or which cannot for reasons be produced in the factories and laboratories of Lunapolis.

"I think I mentioned once that the Neo-men are a going concern. I actually used the term in its most literal sense. That accounts for the mass production of such strange and inconsistent objects as television sets, lighting fixtures, cooking units and the rest. All are sold through dummy concerns on Earth—and I assure you they sell like hotcakes. With their superior abilities to learn and concentrate, Neo-men are able not only to produce better things, but cheaper things as well. A large number of products, which are highly popular and widely advertised on Earth, are the result of Neo-man labor and ingenuity.

"Other dummy concerns buy up the various things needed here, in Lunapolis. There is quite a nice margin of profit in these transactions, and as a result the Neo-man organization is what modestly might be called prosperous. Transportation of freight to and from Earth, of course, is accomplished by de-gravity cruisers. In everything done, in every step from start to finish, the greatest care and secrecy is used. The fact that all these activities haven't been discovered fully attests to the abilities and effectiveness of the Neo-man organization."

Ellen's words left Dall with a feeling of depression. Wonderful though it might be, the Neo-man organization was something he was pledged to destroy. It wasn't this that concerned him so much as the knowledge that doing so would in all probability mean the destruction of Ellen as well. The pride, which she had voiced clearly, showed how inextricably bound up in the Neo-men were her life and hopes.

The other things he saw in the factories and laboratories of Lunapolis, however, strengthened his waning resolve. For even though considered by Ellen as verging on secondary impor-tance, he found war material production taking place on a nevertheless impressive scale. Huge machines whirred and throbbed everywhere; finished products rolled in an apparently endless parade from countless assembly lines; and in every field and branch of activity scientists, engineers, and technicians labored industriously at their multitude of tasks, supervising, checking, designing, experimenting. All were tributaries that fed a mighty mainstream. With smooth, implacable precision, a bewildered variety of machines, equipment, and supplies was being turned out, ranging from degravity cruisers to mess kits.

AS IF this overwhelming display of productivity and ingenuity alone were not enough, Dall was given demonstrations of a few of the more important Neo-man weapons, such as the paralysis beam projector, the static field generator, and the atomic force protection screen. The action of this latter device was shown by means of a motion picture film recording, taken on the surface of the Moon's perpetually hidden side. Dall knew that Earth as yet had found no adequate protection against the atomic bomb. But with a characteristic genius—if the films Dall saw were fully to be credited—the Neo-men had done so.

What few remaining doubts Dall had about the ability of the Neo-men to conquer Earth perished miserably. In his mind stark emphasis was given to the knowledge that Earth's sole hope lay in his efforts to trick Ellen for possession of the Control.

Further sightseeing tours followed, this time through the great, complex network of utility plants that serviced Lunapolis. These were located beneath the city, in vast sub-chambers within the colossal pedestal upon which it rested. The utility plants were in effect the internal organs of Lunapolis. The city itself was the body, of which the Control was the brain. Dall recalled what Jonothan had said about Lunapolis being a mutant city—an entity. He now saw with his own eyes how true this apparently fantastic description was.

Ellen was a charming and highly informative guide. Her knowledge of the city's bewildering intricacies was startling in its broad range and keen grasp of detail. Among the machines and devices that she showed and explained to Dall were those that prepared, distributed, and regulated the city's air, water, light, and heat, and also those which collected and disposed of the city's sewage and other waste matter. He was shown the monster generators that created and maintained the invisible, vast force field over Lunapolis, which prevented the atmosphere from escaping into space. There were other generators that maintained the city's artificial Earth-normal gravity. Most interesting to Dall, however, was the degravity apparatus, which accomplished the raising and lowering of the city within its huge concealing crater shaft.

"What is its purpose anyway?" he asked Ellen. "Why was it necessary to build the city along the general lines of an elevator?"

For one of the few times in which it ever happened, Ellen's lovely features showed mystification. "I wish I were certain, Harvey. The Neo-men aren't the ones who built the city, you know. However, I think the main idea was that of concealment. With the city lowered into the crater, none would ever guess it existed. At any rate, the Neo-men use the apparatus for that purpose. Warning signal devices are constantly in operation. When they detect the approach of a strange vessel, regardless of the direction from which it might come, the city automatically lowered from sight."

ELLEN'S explanation confirmed what Dall had already guessed. He knew the fact that it was more or less a theory reflected no discredit either on her or the Neo-men. They had come to Lunapolis as people of the Middle Ages might have come to a modern city of Earth. They'd had to learn to use the wonderful, highly-advanced machines and devices, and their success spoke volumes for their abilities, though they hadn't discovered the functions or operating principles in every case.

"The Control in particular has baffled us," Ellen told Dall on one occasion. "Actually, years of cautious trial and error experimentation passed before we realized the full scope of its powers. There were a number of near disasters. We now know what the Control can do, but we don't know exactly how it does it. We never dared examine its inner mechanism. An attempt to take it apart might very well result in the total destruction of Lunapolis, just as ignorant surgical tampering with the brain may result in the death both of the brain and the body."

"I've never seen the Control at close range," Dall remarked casually. "It must be an interesting thing to watch."

Ellen nodded. "You'll get your chance, Harvey. I'll take you to the chamber in Capitol Tower where the Control is kept, sometime soon."

The tours about Lunapolis with Ellen were, of course, spread over an extensive interval and took up only a minor part of each day-period. Ellen was greatly occupied with administrative duties, and Dall himself was kept busy in his own line of work. He tried to regard his researches as little more than a subterfuge to occupy his time while he laid the groundwork of his stratagem to get at the Control. But the problems upon which he was engaged proved intensely fascinating. With the enthusiasm of a true scientist, he was becoming engrossed in his work to the exclusion of time, place, and frequently even of the secret ends toward which he was stealthily moving.

Dall saw little of Frontenac. In line with their plans, the other had also taken tests to determine his interests and capabilities. He had qualified as a senior laboratory assistant, but had not been given military rank, something which was accorded only Neo-men. Like Dall, he too was interested in his work; unlike Dall, however, his volatile nature chafed under the restraints of pursuing a single line of activity. Even more than Dall, he regarded his work merely as a temporary stop-gap, and he was becoming impatient to the point of irascibility for the fruition of their scheme.

Out of deference to their friendship, Ellen had allowed Dall and Frontenac to continue sharing the same apartment. They saw each other only for a short while in the morning and in the evening of each day-period. When their daily work-shifts were over, each went his separate way—Dall to keep an appointment with Ellen, and Frontenac to remain inside and read, or to seek such vicarious amusement as was to be found in Neo-man public entertainment centers.

At first Frontenac showed keen interest in the progress of Dall's pretended romance with the Phrenarch of Lunapolis. Each morning he questioned Dall as to what had taken place the preceding night. But lately he had lapsed into a strange silence on the subject. He listened politely to whatever Dall volunteered, but he no longer asked questions of his own.

Dall realized that the other was growing withdrawn, embittered. During their stay in Lunapolis events had led them into treading two widely divergent walks of life. Frontenac was left too much to himself. As a member of the Old Race, he was not accepted into the social circles of his Neo-man co-workers. And while Dall often invited Frontenac to accompany him and Ellen on their evening excursions, the other claimed his presence would only hinder Dall in what he was trying to do.

DALL was painfully aware that he and Frontenac were becoming estranged. Often, as he dressed for a date with Ellen, he caught the other watching him with an expression unmistakably hostile. And in their lessening verbal exchanges, Frontenac was oddly evasive. At last Dall brought the matter directly out into the open.

"Look here, Jules, you've been acting mighty funny lately. Is anything wrong?"

"Wrong?" Frontenac's dark, thin features registered an expression of elaborate perplexity. "I'm afraid I don't know what you mean."

"I'm pretty sure you do. You've been avoiding me and generally acting as if I'd caught something contagious."

"Maybe it's because you have caught something contagious, Harvey—the Neo-man fever. And maybe it's because Mrs. Frontenac's little boy finally woke up to the fact that he's all alone in the world and will have to look out for himself."

"Just what do you mean by that?"

Frontenac threw out his hands in an explosive gesture. "Good Lord, Harvey, do I have to draw you a picture? You and Ellen Pancrest have become so thick, it's being talked about all over Lunapolis."

"So what?" Dall demanded. "It simply means our plan is working better than we ever expected."

"Does it, Harvey? Does it? I'd say it means you've gone over to the Neo-men hide, hair, and soul. And as for the plan, your only interest in it now is most likely as an excuse for seeing Ellen Pancrest. She has you so completely hooked that you don't even know it. Don't try to tell me otherwise—I've been watching you. You've shown all the typical symptoms of a man bit by the love-bug."

Dall glanced away. He said slowly, "I haven't forgotten the plan, Jules. You've got to believe me. I'm still working on it."

"Fine," Frontenac said. "Keep working on it. In the meantime, I'll see what I can do about getting back to Earth alone—before old age sets in."

"Jules—cut it out, will you?" Dall caught the smaller man's shoulders. "I know you haven't been enjoying yourself here, but that's no reason to jump on me with both feet. I said I was working on the plan—and I meant it."

Frontenac shrugged himself loose. "You talk a nice bill of goods, Harvey, but it'll take more than words to convince me. If and when you get hold of the Control, that'll be the day I become interested." He turned and walked from the room. The door closed behind him with an air of finality.

Dall felt chilled. He knew now what had come between Frontenac and himself. And it would have to be through deed rather than word that he would regain the other's faith. But he wondered if, despite his assurances, he would be able to accomplish the deed. He had to admit that most if not all the things that Frontenac had said about Ellen had an uncomfortably large basis in truth.

IT WAS all too easy—dangerously easy, in fact—to regard Ellen with feelings that were deeper and more poignant than those of mere attraction. He had learned long ago that there were two entirely different sides to her nature. One was that as the Phrenarch of Lunapolis, cold, business-like, frequently arrogant and domineering. The other was that as Ellen Pancrest, warm, sympathetic, and unaffected. It was this side of her that had led him to the verge of traitorhood. She was all woman, lovely, exceptionally talented, and with a mind whose most subtle shadings often merged harmoniously with his. He was startled at times by the recurrent discovery of how alike they were in so many ways. They shared the same interests, had the same viewpoints and opinions. Only in their objectives regarding the Neo-men and the Old Race was there any essential difference between them. And even this, Dall realized with dismay, had begun to fade with time, constant contact with the Neo-men, and the spell of Ellen's personality.

He became sharply aware that his feelings for Ellen had reached a point where they might very well make impossible the completion of his plans. Earth depended on him—even if un-knowingly—for help against the Neo-men. Conquest had to be avoided at any cost. Jonothan, that mysterious and god-like being, had had strong reasons for wanting to prevent it. And he had died for his beliefs. When all this was weighed in the balance, Dall realized that his feelings for Ellen paled into in-significance. He knew the only possible course he could take. Yet he wondered if he would be able to follow it unwaveringly to its inevitable and tragic end.

Events with Ellen followed the usual pattern, though Dall continued to grapple with his problem. He was careful to reveal nothing of his inner turmoil. It was extremely difficult, for his daily contacts with Ellen and Frontenac kept reminding him of the two conflicting poles between which he was torn. Since his showdown with Frontenac, their relationship had grown even more strained. The mercurial little man had shut himself behind an unyielding wall of cold and silent aloofness. The contrast with Ellen's warmth and vivacity was painful.

One evening, however, when Dall went to keep a dinner date at Ellen's apartment, he found her tense with excitement. She had dressed as exquisitely as always, and with her flushed cheeks and shining eyes, she made a vital and compelling figure.

"Harvey, a report from Earth reached me today that the political situation has grown enormously worse. War is expected to break out at any time within the next few weeks." The news had burst out of her. She paused a moment as though to catch her breath.

Dall waited, cold and empty with despair. He knew what was coming even before the girl spoke again.

"You know, Harvey, that the Neo-men are determined to stop that war. Accordingly, we don't intend to sit back and let it happen. Word has been sent to our agents in the various governments of Earth to prepare for action. The Neo-man fleet and army here, in Lunapolis, are being mobilized and equipped for duty. Within several days at the most we shall be ready."

CHAPTER TWENTY

AGAIN Dall struggled to keep his emotions from betraying him. The effort wasn't entirely necessary, however; Ellen was lost in thought. Her green eyes glowed as though reflecting some wonderful inner wisdom. What that was Dall soon learned.

Ellen spoke abruptly, her voice vibrant. "The time has come, Harvey! The Neo-men are moving forward to meet their destiny. Nothing will be able to stop them—nothing! It won't be much longer until they win their rightful places in the world. And then—and then, Harvey—Earth will be swept clean of war, incompetence, and corruption. The Neo-men will bring a true Golden Age!"

Some of her fire touched Dall. It wasn't wholly a clever act that brought an expression of sympathetic interest to his face.

Suddenly, impulsively, Ellen caught at his arms. "And think, Harvey, you'll be a part of it! You'll have a hand in shaping the future history of Earth. Within your lifetime you'll see the Earth become a better, happier place. You'll see it made new, clean, and beautiful. That will be something, won't it, Harvey?"

"It certainly will."

"And afterward, Harvey...afterward—" She broke off, her long lashes dropping to veil her eyes. After a moment she laughed. "But I'm getting too far ahead of things. Right now dinner is waiting—and I'm starved!"

Ellen was gay and voluble during the meal. Dall forced himself to respond to her mood, though his emotions surged turbulently. Bitter within him was the knowledge that he had finally to make the supreme decision. He told himself it had happened too soon. He wished he'd been allowed a little more time. He didn't want the happiness he'd known with Ellen to end so quickly.

When the dinner was finished Ellen rose, her green eyes sparkling. "This is an important occasion, Harvey. Let's think of a really unusual way to spend the evening. What do you suggest?"

"Uhm-m-m…" Dall rubbed his jaw, frowning in mock-solemnity. Inwardly he was tense and cold, filled with dull, heavy pain. At last he snapped his fingers. "I've got it! A while back you promised to show me the Control. Suppose we pay it a visit? That should be unusual enough."

Ellen nodded her gold-brown head without hesitation. "All right, Harvey. Give me a few minutes to get ready." She turned and hurried from the room.

The Control, Dall found shortly, was kept in a large, severely plain chamber high in Capitol Tower. A special elevator led up to that floor. Guards were on duty at both ends of the elevator shaft, and there were more guards within the chamber itself.

THE Control rested upon an octagonal, gleaming metal pedestal that rose approximately to shoulder height. The chamber was bare of all else. There was no machinery, nothing in the way of furniture or other decorations. Nor were there any windows. Cold, hard metal sheathed the entire room with the thoroughness of a bank vault. Illumination was provided by light brackets spaced around the walls.

Ellen spoke a few words of dismissal to the captain of the guards. He saluted, and then, issuing crisp orders, he marched his detail from the room. The ponderous metal doors closed. With a shock, Dall realized that he and Ellen were alone.

She smiled and gestured at the Control. "Now, Harvey, you can be just as curious as you please."

She led the way to the pedestal. Amid a silence that had all the quality of awed wonder, she and Dall stood gazing at the Control.

Within the transparent, square crystal case the bewilderingly intricate mechanism that somehow gave the Control its state of uncanny pseudo-life moved with enigmatic activity. Countless multi-colored, tiny lights flickered and darted within the device, appearing and vanishing in a constant, kaleidoscopic change and interplay of hues. The phenomenon had a kind of frenetic tempo that held the eyes hypnotically.

Dall felt nervous tension build up within him. The Control was within his reach at last. It was the only thing that now would stop the Neo-men in their preparations for the conquest of Earth. All he had to do was reach out and take it. Yet he hesitated. And hesitating, he wondered if he would be able to go through with it after all.

He became aware that Ellen had turned to glance at him. He was unable to prevent the involuntary, conscience-stricken jerk with which he responded to the motion. In an attempt to cover up, he grasped at the first thing that came to his mind. But even as he put his thoughts into words, he wondered if his ruse weren't merely an effort to postpone what he knew was clearly and inescapably his duty.

"How is the Control able to operate in a place like this?" he asked, gesturing around the chamber.

"It can operate anywhere in Lunapolis," Ellen returned. "Metal walls or other obstructions make no difference. As to why this should be, the prevailing theory among Neo-man scientists is that the Control somehow functions through the medium of hyperspace. This medium links the Control to the various machines and devices, which it operates in somewhat the same manner that the nerves of the body link the brain to the various muscles and organs. But since distance is no factor in hyperspace, the Control might be described as being in *direct* contact with every machine and device—simultaneously a part of all—in a way that makes the nerves of the body crude and cumbersome by contrast."

Ellen's voice went into silence. Only dimly was Dall aware of it; his eyes were fixed in dread fascination upon the Control.

Now, he thought. *Now!* All he had to do was to take a step forward, reach out with his hands—and the Control would be his. In an act requiring only a fraction of time he would be master of everyone and everything in Lunapolis. His power would be practically limitless, his will supreme. He would be able to destroy or let stand as the whim moved him.

HIS muscles tensed. Only a step forward. It required hardly any energy. It could be done in a split-second. Ellen wouldn't realize what was happening until the Control was in his hands.

Just a step... His muscles were bunched, quivering. Perspiration beaded his forehead. Perspiration was moist and clammy on his palms.

He couldn't move. It was as though another will was superimposed on his, making movement impossible.

How long he stood there, straining but immobile, he never knew. All eternity could have passed. All the people who had ever existed and who had still to exist could have paraded one by one before him.

At last he relaxed, the breath sighing hopelessly from his lips. He felt exhausted, sick-defeated.

It was impossible. He couldn't do it. That single step forward had proved too much after all.

Ellen had won.

"Harvey..."

Ellen's voice. Ellen's hand on his arm. He turned his head to look at her—and his mind exploded nova-like under the impact of his discovery. He was suddenly and devastatingly weak, shaken to the very nucleus of his being.

For Ellen—*knew!*

Her green eyes swam mistily in tears, and tears beaded her long lashes like tiny globules of crystal, shining prismatically in the pulsing, many-hued light from the Control. But she was smiling, a smile of utter, intense joy.

"Harvey, you didn't...you didn't..." Her voice caught, broke. Then it came again, strengthening. "Harvey, all this—

the visit to the Control—was arranged as a test. I wanted so much to believe in your loyalty. But I couldn't take a chance, knowing what I did of your background and character. There was too much at stake. I didn't want to doubt you—but nothing could be overlooked that might interfere with the Neomen and their plans.

"You see, Harvey, I noticed your reaction to the announcement I made a while ago. And then—and then you suggested a visit to the Control. When I left you to get ready, I took a certain precaution. The Control you see here isn't the real one. It's a fake—like the one with which I tricked Melgard."

Her words added to Dall's chaotic stupefaction. He said numbly:

"A…fake?"

"Yes, Harvey. But now—now you shall see the genuine Control. You have proved yourself. I shall keep my promise." Radiant with her inner fire of gladness and relief, she turned toward the doors of the chamber and called out what was evidently a prearranged signal.

As Dall watched dazedly, the doors opened. The captain of the guards entered the room, grinning. In his hands he held a transparent, square crystal case similar in appearance to the one now on the pedestal. But the varicolored motes or radiance within this were many times brighter, their activity more intense. And the case emanated power. Dall felt it as unmistakably as a glow of heat from a blast furnace.

TAKING the imitation from the pedestal, the captain of the guards replaced it with the real Control. Then he snapped to attention, saluted, and strode from the room. Once more the heavy doors closed.

"Harvey…" Ellen's voice again.

Unreal, far-off, like something in a dream. "Harvey, look at me. You aren't angry, are you? It seems such a cheap trick now. Forgive me, Harvey. Please say you forgive me."

"Forgive you?" Dall muttered. His eyes went slowly to the Control, glowing, pulsing, filling the metal-sheathed severity of the chamber with faint, soft chromatic light. He felt its power again. It seemed to warm him, to give him strength. His mind was suddenly clear. Everything became sharp and in focus, so bright, so vivid, it registered almost as pain. His glance returned to Ellen.

"Forgive you?" he said again. He nodded gravely. "Yes, I forgive you."

Something moved in her face. It was queerly as if her features were a reflection in water of exceptional clarity and a finger had disturbed its surface. And then, abruptly, she was close against him, her arms encircling and straining tight, her face pressed to his chest. His own arms came up, hesitated, then went around her.

After a while she stirred. She raised her face to his. Her lips moved in a slow smile, tremulous and misty, eloquent with its eternal message.

"You've never kissed me, Harvey…"

He found her lips without knowing how it happened. The chamber became still.

And then she drew away. Dall took a deep breath. His surroundings were even more vivid now. Each item, each detail, registered with a steel-sharp diamond-bright perfection. He said gently:

"That was farewell, Ellen."

The green eyes widened in perplexity. "Farewell…?"

In another moment she understood. Her neck muscles corded for a scream, but even before sound could issue from her throat, Dall was moving with that superhuman speed that had come to him on two occasions before.

One step forward—and he had the Control. He held it tightly and tensely in his hands. He looked at Ellen. His face was—different. He wasn't quite Harvey Dall. He was a personality of scope above and beyond his normal self.

Violent, mind-wrenching shock, penetrating in all its catastrophic implications, robbed Ellen of the strength to complete her scream. She stared into Dall's eyes for a long moment before she could make a sound. And then it was only a whisper that issued from her bloodless lips.

"Harvey—you…you took the Control."

"Yes, Ellen. Your doubt showed you consider the Neo-men and their plans more important than I. Looking at it the other way around, the Old Race and its freedom are more important than you. So I took the Control. I couldn't have missed a chance for my side any more than you were willing to take a risk for yours."

SHE nodded ever so slightly. For an instant a reluctant admiration struggled with the despairing horror in her face. Then her wildness faded; sanity and self-possession came. Something of fear remained in her rigid green gaze, but it was an impersonal fear, defiant. On the verge of certain defeat though she might be, she was neither abject nor hysterical. Her voice was stronger, almost normal, when she spoke again.

"What do you intend to do, Harvey? What are you planning?"

"The Old Race must be left alone," Dall returned, with quiet emphasis. "To make absolutely certain of that, I'm going to destroy every weapon in Lunapolis, and every laboratory, factory, machine, and supply used to make weapons. And then Frontenac and I return to Earth—in a degravity cruiser, of course, one of which I shall leave for that purpose…

"Something you haven't discovered, Ellen, is that I'm a special operative of the United States Secret Service. My report on the Neo-men will bring quick action. Your agents will be weeded out from their government hiding places. And when they've been made powerless to interfere, news of the Neo-men and their plans will be given to the entire world. The Neo-man organization on Earth will collapse. The element of surprise on which you counted so heavily will be gone forever."

"But…but do you intend to leave everyone in Lunapolis completely helpless?"

"Long enough to let their lesson sink in. Later a rescue expedition will come from Earth. We'll have degravity cruisers, you know. And I think I'll take the Control with me in case there are any hard feelings. Functioning through hyperspace, the distance should have practically no effect on its operations."

"And the impending atomic war on Earth, Harvey? What about that?"

"I intend to take with me plans and models of your weapons. One of them will be the atomic force protection screen."

Ellen slumped, rallied. But she couldn't overcome the hopelessness that showed in her features.

Dall watched her, hesitating, compassion a dark shadow in his eyes. Then his shoulders squared. Lines of strain deepening whitely around his mouth, he looked intently, purposefully, at the radiant crystal case in his hands.

"Harvey—wait!" Ellen's cry tore knife-like into the silence.

Involuntarily Dall looked up.

"Think, Harvey—think. Lunapolis and the Control are a single entity. Do you suppose that entity will answer a command to destroy itself? Do you suppose it will submit to destroying even so much as part of itself? No, Harvey, it will refuse, even as a coldly rational human being would refuse. And that refusal will come in terms of living, terrible force, annihilating the one who gives that outrageous command."

Cold of death touched Dall. His metal-gray eyes probed fiercely into the vehement green ones.

"It's a lie," he said at last. "A trick."

She shook her head slowly, sadly. "It happened once before, Harvey. A long time ago, when my father and the first settlers in Lunapolis discovered what the Control was and what it could do. One of those early Neo-men wasn't in sympathy with my father and the others. He seized the Control and tried to destroy the city. But the Control…exterminated him. The Control and the forces it operates can be used against individuals or groups within the city—but not against the city itself."

"Clever," Dall breathed. Mere bravado—empty, meaningless. For in his mind was the impulse that would send his thoughts arrowing into the Control—and he hesitated.

"It's true, Harvey," Ellen insisted passionately. "Every word of what I said is true. What you plan to do means suicide."

Once more deathly cold touched Dall. Was the girl actually sincere? If she was, he realized that he faced stalemate—defeat.

CHAPTER TWENTY-ONE

A WAVE of unreasoning anger swept abruptly over Dall. His lips writhed in a soundless snarl of defiance. Almost savagely he directed his furious gaze at the Control.

"No, Harvey! *Don't!*" Ellen ran at him frantically.

And then—it happened.

"Harvey Dall—attention! Concentrate now. You must link your mind with mine."

A voice—but an eerily silent voice. A purely mental voice like the one Dall had experienced twice before. He stiffened under the electrifying shock of it. But he wasn't quite Harvey Dall, and his surprise was gone almost in the same instant that it came. And before Ellen, already in motion, could reach him, he stretched a mental hand to the warm, firm, and friendly one that came swiftly and surely to meet it.

The Control—*awoke.*

Like a smoldering ember compared to a forest fire was its former radiance to that which blazed from it now. Light, intense and with all the rich hues of the spectrum, filled the chamber. And from somewhere came a vast, deep organ note of sound, a mighty vibration that seemed to reverberate within the very structure of matter itself. Through the chamber it thundered—through and beyond, as though to the ultimate end of the Universe.

Ellen stopped. It was as if a huge, invisible hand had gripped her. And like a hand it held her helpless.

Somehow, with a knowledge not his own, Dall knew that similar hands had gripped all over Lunapolis. Like Ellen, Neomen everywhere in the city were being stopped in whatever they were doing. An all-pervading, supernal force was keeping them immobile. Imprisoned—entranced—they waited frozenly for what was to come.

Throughout the chamber, throughout the city, the vast organ note throbbed again.

Dall was rigid, his eyes fixed and glassy. It was less than a man who stood there, holding the Control. It was a shell—a conductor. For through his mind as through an electric cable a current of mental force poured into the Control, giving directions of incomprehensible magnitude and complexity. For the first time in too long the Control was being used as its creators had meant it to be used. It was being...played. A rare old violin, made by the hands of a master craftsman, reveals little of its true beauty of tone, its full musical potentialities, when played by an amateur. But in the hands of a practiced artist it becomes an instrument capable of scaling the heights and plumbing the depths of the human soul.

The Control was being played... Its mighty organ notes beat and thundered throughout every part and particle of Lunapolis.

THE ponderous metal doors of the chamber swung open. A man entered, striding forward with swift, eager steps; a tall, slender man with a thick mane of snow-white hair framing a pale, ascetic face. His dark eyes were vivid by contrast, deep pools of strength and wisdom, hypnotic in their intensity.

The newcomer came to a stop before Dall. He smiled and extended his hands. With the unhesitating deliberation of an automaton, Dall placed within them the Control.

"Thank you, Harvey Dall."

Awareness, the fire of self-will, flickered and then leaped into fullness within Dall's eyes. He stared at the tall, white-haired man. He gasped under the impact of recognition, stunned, incredulous.

"Jonothan!" he burst out. "Jonothan!"

"Yes."

"But...but you're dead. I saw Melgard shoot at you. I saw you die."

"What you saw was an illusion, a sort of mass hallucination, which I created by mental projection. Melgard had seen me. If I were to be of any further usefulness to you, he had to be tricked into thinking I was dead. I did not know at the time what shape future events would take. The action seemed necessary in view of the possibility that Melgard might remain in power."

Dall shook his head ruefully. "I should have known better than to have thought Melgard could catch you so easily." He met the quiet smile in Jonothan's dark eyes. An abrupt thought made him stiffen. "You were the one who kept me from spoiling everything by jumping at the imitation Control a while back. I see it now. I thought it was due to weakness on my part."

Jonothan nodded. "I had been keeping what might be called a mental eye on the progress of affairs between you and Ellen Pancrest. I knew that she planned to test you, and I saw to it that you were warned of the trick she had prepared. Since I had been keeping secretly in the background, I did so in a way that would not reveal my existence to you. I intended to save that for a more crucial moment."

"But if I had known you were still alive..."

"I know what is in your mind, Harvey Dall. Hastening matters to spare you of your present feelings for Ellen Pancrest might have led to disaster. I saw that you were following a course that had the greatest opportunity of success. I decided to keep my existence unknown to you. Regardless of the emotional entanglements into which you were falling, success was the only important thing."

Jonothan paused, and momentarily the warm fingers of his thoughts seemed to draw away. He looked down at the Control; sternness came into his pale, slim face.

The mighty organ note throbbed. Dall felt the warm mental fingers again, interlocking firmly with his. He had a startling vision. The impenetrable, steel-sheathed chamber was gone. Through a kind of luminous gray fog, he saw the Neo-man hosts of Lunapolis. They stood in a vast circle about Jonothan, Ellen, and himself, a great ring of silent, motionless, watching faces. Dall saw them with a strange clarity. It was as if some vast and intricate warping of space had eliminated all differences in distance and perspective, making each individual wherever in Lunapolis he might be a part of the whole.

BEYOND the surrounding mass of faces Dall could see nothing. There was only the gray fog, vague and featureless. And with the countless watching faces shining through the fog, the entire scene was oddly unreal—dreamlike.

The faces waited, watching. The faces of puppets they were, expressionless, mask-like, dominated by a superhuman will.

Somehow Dall knew this was the truth. But he sensed that it wasn't Jonothan's unaided will alone that held the populace of the city in thrall; rather it was Jonathan's will increased and intensified enormously by the powers of the Control. For the Control was more than merely a device that responded to human thought; it was an instrument capable of playing cosmic music. And it was in the hands of a master virtuoso, who could play symphonies that could crumble the very foundations of matter, that could twist and tear the very fabric of space; symphonies that annihilated time and distance, that held human lives in trance-like bondage.

It was this that explained the sternness of Jonathan's features. He was asserting his complete mastery over everyone in Lunapolis. He was a being whose nature rebelled violently against even the mere thought of causing pain and harm. But through the aid of the Control he was above the limits of his most deep-rooted instincts. He was truly god-like now. If forced to do so, he would destroy without hesitation or scruple.

Dall realized this clearly. He accepted it without reservation, as something entirely natural and consistent. And he knew that the watching wraith-faces accepted it, too.

A reverberating throb from the organ-voice. Jonothan looked up. The sternness went from his face. It took on a deep calm. His dark eyes gazed out over the enrapt assemblage, the people of Lunapolis who, though they looked like nothing so much as spectres from some astral region, were present as surely as if in the flesh. He spoke. His mental voice reached out to every nook and corner of all the vast city, penetrating easily and surely into every mind. It held a deep, sonorous quality. And it chanted as a bard of old might have chanted the stirring verses of a mighty epic.

CHAPTER TWENTY-TWO

JONOTHAN spoke. "Listen to that which I am here to tell you, for it is something to which your self-conceit and vainglory have made you blind. Listen—and heed.

"In the beginning was the people who are known to you as the Old Race. It was their nature that they should be treacherous and filled with greed. It was their nature that they should commit murder and theft, and create untold harm and loss in the name of causes and ideals, which to them seemed just and good. But among them even in the darkest times was organization and laws under which good managed to flourish among evil. And thus this people whom we shall call the Old Race grew in numbers and advanced along civilization's tedious road. Often they fell behind. Sometimes, for long periods, they stopped along the way. Yet always there would be a resurgence of movement, a rebirth, and they went on.

"When this people whom we term the Old Race reached a certain point in the road, their progress began to grow increasingly more rapid. Before long they were striding with the steps of giants. They harnessed the wind, water, fire, and even the lightnings that struck down from the sky. In their machines they traveled swiftly and effortlessly over the surface of the world, and through the very air itself. With their devices they communicated with each other over great distances. Their instruments probed the secrets of the farthest stars and magnified into visibility the most minute virus. They were taking the first feeble steps that would eventually launch them into space. They penetrated even to the secret of the atom itself, and with their knowledge came into possession of forces terrible enough to devastate the entire planet.

"There was better organization, better laws, and there was more good for all. But even among their wonderworking machines and instruments, the men of the Old Race were not happy. Something was lacking. There was a feeling of insecurity. There was growing distrust, growing discontent, among groups and nations. There was increasing pessimism, apathy, and restlessness, all of which made themselves felt in a widespread degeneration of minds, morals, and institutions.

"A few with vision realized the trouble. Mentally and spiritually the Old Race hasn't kept pace with its scientific progress. For all their splendid machines and cities the men of the Old Race were still creatures of the wilderness. Only in the wilderness were they truly happy. Always, if not chained financially and socially to the cities, they sought the wilderness. It supplied something lacking in the cities.

"It was something that the men of the Old Race did not themselves understand. They knew it vaguely as a wanderlust, a desire 'to get away from it all.'

"In their discontent and blind striving the men of the Old Race have down through the ages looked forward to the coming of a Savior, or to the dawning of a Golden Age. They searched for a Shangri-La and absorbed themselves in the long-gone glories of a mythical Atlantis. What they actually yearned for was unity and harmony, with their fellows and with the civilization they had built, and they gave this yearning various idealized explanations, none of which were close to the truth. They did not realize that their desires for betterment and improvement would come from *within themselves.*

"At present the Old Race regards atomic weapons as indefensible. The people whom we shall call the Neo-men have discovered a defense. In the future even more terrible weapons will be devised, and defenses against them. But the only true defense against weapons, against war, will come from *within the race itself.*

"And it has come."

JONOTHAN paused; the organ-note boomed. Then the chant went on.

"Through its striving for improvement, for unity and content, the Old Race as a whole has produced within itself titanic pressures, which have been working subconsciously to mold it into something better. Gradually, but with a pace now increasing, the Old Race is evolving into Neo-men, a people more fully adjusted to the problems and demands of city life. But the Neo-men are not the final solution. Despite their superior abilities, they have all the faults and flaws of the Old Race, many of them greatly magnified. Were the Neo-men the final solution, there would still be war—but war employing weapons as tremendously more lethal than the atomic as these themselves are more lethal than swords. The race would come to an end in one brief cataclysm that would rock the very Universe.

"But the Neo-men are not the final solution. For from them as Neo-men from the Old Race has come the people whom we shall term the Ultra-men, and by almost the same process of evolution. There is a difference—but a difference only of degree.

"The dim, blind struggles for improvement within the Old Race, given force and direction by the mass subconscious mind, created the changes in the germ plasm that produced the Neo-men. This mass mind could not conceive of beings higher in the scale of evolution than the Neo-man, but in them it furnished a springboard from which still greater improvement was to come. Within Neo-men themselves the desire for betterment went on. Possessed of keen, swift minds, the Neo-men mass subconscious possessed even more force and direction than that of the Old Race. Though fewer Neo-men were in existence, the power of each individual mind was many times greater. As a whole, Neo-man mass subconscious mind possessed sufficient power capable of producing the further changes in the germ plasm necessary to create the Ultra-men.

"Though possessed of enormous intelligence, new senses, and vast bodily improvements, the Ultra-men represented the first great change for the better chiefly because of one certain trait. They were a people to whom the entire conception of war was alien and repulsive. They were unable to do even so much as think of causing harm to an individual or group without violent emotional reactions. Thus the Ultra-men represented that stage in the evolution of the race where war, strife, and conflict of all kinds finally come to all end; where civilization is based on peace, intelligence, and truth.

"It was the Ultra-men who built Lunapolis. They left Earth for almost exactly the same reasons as did the Neo-men. They discovered the degravity principle of interspace propulsion at a time when the first crude aircraft had still to be built. They were happy in Lunapolis, but eventually they…left. The desire for improvement had not died out with them. Though fewer in numbers than even the Neo-men, the power of their minds was even greater. Telepathic, they were able to join forces and do *consciously* what previously had been a product of the racial mass mind working subconsciously.

"The Ultra-men evolved the final, one-remaining step, producing the beings whom, merely for a convenient terminology, we shall call the Ultimates. The Ultimates were beyond the need for cities; the Universe itself was their home. They possessed qualities and attributes that are impossible even for me to describe.

"LUNAPOLIS was left intact for those additional Ultra-men who had still to evolve. It was not suspected that science would make such great strides that the Neo-men would be able to reach the Moon before they had reached the proper stage of evolution. But even so nothing had been left to chance; for to me was given the duty of remaining behind as a guardian and guide.

"It was chiefly through scientific curiosity that I permitted the Neo-men to take the steps that finally placed the entire evolutionary process in grave danger. When I realized the extent and significance of this danger, it was too late to take the simple, immediate procedures necessary to circumvent it. The Control, which would have enabled me to take quick and effective counter-measures, was kept under heavy guard. My powers, of course, are limited in that it is impossible for me to do anything that would cause death or hurt to a living creature. The Ultimates would not have aided me; they were above the petty problems of race. The Control would have overcome these drawbacks—but I had first to gain possession of it.

"Thus it was that I selected Harvey Dall as a champion or agent to do that which I was unable to accomplish personally. And I chose him not merely because he had carried his rocket researches to the point of success, despite constant and serious handicaps placed in his way by the Neo-men, but because he alone possessed the strength of mind and the integrity of character necessary to carry out a truly herculean task. That he won out in the end is due not so much to the shrewdness of my choice or to such comparatively feeble help as I was able to give, but to the fact that his courage and honor were even greater than I had estimated."

Jonothan turned to smile at Dall. Swift protest stirred in Dall's mind.

"No—the credit is something I don't deserve. I…I was weak."

"But you won, Harvey Dall. In your weakness, it seems, is your greatest strength."

Jonothan returned his attention to the ghostly assemblage. The organ note sounded again; the current of Jonothan's thoughts resumed, grim, measured.

"Now it is possible for me to prevent what may in the end have very well resulted in catastrophe for the race. In their plans to uplift and improve the Old Race through conquest, Neo-men made the serious error of assuming that their superiority of intelligence furnished them with all the justification required. They were wrong. As throughout all history, they were a few who, in the name of a mistaken ideals and causes, were capable of creating great harm.

"FOR the Old Race was being not merely underestimated; it was hardly regarded as being an important factor at all. That was almost fatally wrong. The Old Race is inferior to the Neo-men only in that they learn more slowly and possess greater nervous instability. But they learn. And when they set their minds on a task, their persistence is something that raises them above the level of nerves. Though conquered by the Neo-men, they would fight for freedom as they have fought down through the ages. They would fight with a relentless single-mindedness of purpose frightening in its sheer tenacity. Slowly but surely they would learn the secrets of Neo-man science. Slowly but surely they would learn the secrets of Neo-man weapons. And then would come war—war employing devices of such appalling destructiveness that the supernal fires of the Sun itself would pale by comparison.

"That must not be. The race is still evolving. It must not perish before it has finished its climb to perfection. Old Race, Neo-men, Ultra-men—each is nothing more than a step along the way. Neither is the final product of evolution. And since all inevitably travel the same path, it is just as unnecessary to help those in a lower stage of progress as it is unfair to hinder them.

"The Neo-men must abandon their plans of conquest. For unknowingly it is evolution itself that they seek to conquer, and if they win, it will be at the cost of those to come. That is too big a price. The race as a whole is greater than the sum of its parts.

"The Neo-men came from Earth. Back to Earth they must go. And they must go in peace, for it is only in peace that they will remain. They must work side by side with the Old Race. Both have a common destiny, a common goal. Hand in hand they must go forward to meet it.

"There will be suspicion and distrust. There will be conflicts and misunderstandings. The Old Race, too, believes in its complete supremacy. Disenchantment will come hard. But the Old Race learns even if slowly. Before long it will accept the fact of its comparative unimportance in the racial scheme. And before long it will accept the Neo-men as children to trust rather than strangers to fear.

"There will bloody strife. But if in the beginning the Neo-men have made their bid for peace, it will be the strife of groups rather than species. And in degravity cruisers the race will spread out to the planets. Regardless of the potency of weapons to come, it will be too diffused to exterminate utterly. Somewhere, always, the race will go on. Somewhere, always, the race will evolve."

Momentarily Jonothan's thoughts faded. The organ-note throbbed; a ripple seemed to spread through the luminous fog-veil behind which stood the silent spectre gathering. Then Jonothan's thoughts came again, stronger, more emphatic, grim with finality.

"The principle of the degravity cruisers, as well as that of the various Ultra-man machines and instruments that have been fathomed, are now a part of Neo-man knowledge and cannot be taken away. They shall be considered a gift. But Lunapolis has proved its dangerous potentialities. The city, therefore, must go.

"The Neo-men must leave. They will be given three day-periods, as they reckon time, to prepare for the exodus. Only that which is personal or which will prove of benefit to the Old Race may be taken. All weapons, all military devices and equipment, must remain behind. I shall be watching to see that my orders are carried out.

"My message has been given. Heed it—and farewell."

DALL felt Jonothan's mental fingers tighten briefly. Jonothan's thoughts reached him again, but with a quality that indicated they were intended for him alone.

"Farewell, Harvey Dall. To you I give my eternal gratitude—but it is as nothing to the gratitude of the race. You have met your tests bravely. In the years to come there will be further tests. I hope—I know—that you will meet them just as bravely."

"But you, Jonothan," Dall said quickly. "What will you do now?"

"My duties haven't ended, Harvey Dall. They have begun. Ultra-men still exist. They have simply gone to live in a place as remote as the Moon once was. Now I go to join them. And Lunapolis goes with me. Once more—farewell."

Dall nodded slowly—reluctantly. "Yes, Jonothan...farewell."

The Ultra-man smiled for the last time and turned his intense dark eyes upon the Control. The all-pervading organ-sound thundered; the already supernal brilliance of the Control flared higher. The immediate space in which Jonothan stood seemed comprehensibly, eye-wrenchingly, to twist on itself. In the next instant Jonothan and the Control were gone.

The encircling mass of special Neo-men went too. The metal walls of the chamber leaped back into solidity. Once again Dall and Ellen were alone.

He turned anxiously to the girl. Life was creeping back into her green eyes. After a moment she stared at him numbly. Then she turned to glance quickly about the stark emptiness of the chamber. Her gaze lingered on the pedestal. Slowly she turned back to Dall.

"The Control—it's gone! Then...then everything that happened was real."

"Real, Ellen."

"But, Harvey, it means…it means…" Her voice shattered on a sob. Her face writhed and her green eyes strained wide—bright and wild. Abruptly she turned and ran from the chamber.

"Ellen!" Dall cried. "Wait!"

Her racing figure didn't stop; it vanished through the still open doors that led out to the hall. Dall started after the girl. He caught sight of her again. She was running toward the elevators. He increased his pace to overtake her.

The guards who lined the hall on each side stared after him in dazed perplexity. The shock of their experience had evidently not yet worn off. They held their weapons as though they had forgotten that such existed. They made no move to stop Dall.

As she reached the elevators, Ellen suddenly became aware that Dall had followed. She watched him approach, her green eyes swimming in tears. She held her lower lip tightly between her teeth in a futile effort to check the great sobs that shook her.

A moment she stood there, tense, statuesque. Then she whirled in a furiously impulsive movement, snatching a rifle from the hands of a startled guard. She leveled the rifle grimly at Dall.

Shock brought him to an abrupt stop little more than a dozen paces away. There was no fear at what he saw in the girl's face. There was only hurt and a sudden, great tiredness.

"You!" Ellen spat. "You're the one who did it! You're the one who ruined everything—all the Neo-men have worked for."

Dall said heavily, "It was my duty, Ellen."

She laughed shortly, in bitter contempt. "Your duty as a spy and a traitor. Well, as a spy and a traitor, you die!" The muzzle of the rifle centered with lethal directness at Dall's chest. Her finger began to pale with pressure on the trigger.

CHAPTER TWENTY-THREE

DALL stood quietly. He wondered why fear didn't come. He wondered why there was no feeling at all. The answer came to him suddenly—he was already dead. The searing hatred in Ellen's face had killed him more surely than would the stream of tungsten-steel pellets she was shortly to unloose.

Ellen—hesitated. Her eyes widened as though for the first time full realization had come of what she intended to do. And then her finger relaxed on the trigger of the rifle. A convulsive shudder wracked her. In the next instant she swayed; the weapon dropped from her hands. She stared at Dall in plaintive surprise.

"Why, Harvey, I was going to... But...but I couldn't kill you, Harvey. I couldn't!"

A blur of motion. Without knowing how it came about, Dall found Ellen in his arms.

Further surprises were in store for Dall. Ellen recovered so completely from the shock of defeat that it was as though nothing at all had happened. The dreams of the Neo-men became a closed chapter. She put them away as utterly as a gown no longer in fashion. Dall knew that the advanced minds of the Neo-men gave them great powers of adaptability, but he was astonished to learn, particularly in Ellen's case, how great those actually could be. True enough, regret tinged her tones when she spoke of leaving Lunapolis, but always eagerness would come at her mentions of Earth.

With the great majority of Neo-men it was the same. At first it had been difficult for them to believe that their uncanny mental experiences under the influence of Jonothan and the Control had been more than just a dream. But proof of cold, sober reality was amply supplied. For at frequent intervals a mighty organ-note would thunder in warning reminder throughout Lunapolis. And when any Neo-men tried stealthily to hide away in his baggage weapons or information pertaining to weapons, the offender was promptly and painfully chastised. Jonothan, from whatever strange realm into which he had vanished, was watching.

None could have been more excited and enthusiastic about the return to Earth than Frontenac. The volatile scientific-dilettante had been verging almost on a breakdown with the intensity of his loneliness and homesickness. Dall realized that it was this more than anything else that had inspired Frontenac's denunciations. Following Dall's almost personal victory over the Neo-men, Frontenac had been abject in his apologies. Dall had accepted these wholeheartedly and even gratefully.

THE three-day periods that Jonothan had allotted for the exodus from Lunapolis drew to a close. With little more to gather and pack away than their personal belongings, these had been more than sufficient for the Neo-men. The fleet of degravity cruisers was ready, and even before the expiration of the time limits Jonothan had set, they took off. The sleek, slim vessels were a magnificent sight as they rose effortlessly in formation, gleaming in the sunlight, and pointed their tapering bows toward Earth.

In one of the cruisers Dall stood at a viewport with Ellen, gazing down at Lunapolis. The city was receding with distance, becoming toy-like. Its shining perfection was a startling contrast to the dead, pitted landscape of the moon.

The fleet was still on the hidden side, but was moving away with increasing rapidity as acceleration mounted. Before long astronomers on Earth would catch sight of it. The presence of so many ships would have been hard to miss. As events later showed, the fleet was sighted, and the news of its approach was enough to bring a stunned halt to the frantic preparations for war that were taking place. Nor were these preparations resumed afterward—perhaps because of certain plans and instructions given by the Neo-men to the government of every nation.

Dall wasn't concerned about the future just then, however. He was staring intently at the dwindling outlines of Lunapolis.

"Do you really think it'll happen, Harvey?" Frontenac's voice broke a long silence. He was standing before another viewport a short distance away.

Dall nodded. "I'm pretty sure it will, Jules. Keep watching."

The towers and spires of Lunapolis receded with distance, becoming indistinguishable in the dazzle of the Sun's radiance. And then, when the city had the size and general appearance of an alabaster crown, it rose suddenly from the surface of the Moon. Out of the vast crater-mouth it rose, borne by the tremendous column upon which it rested. Higher it lifted, and higher, moving in a direction opposite to that of the fleet. It faded to a glinting mote that vanished among the blazing stars of space.

The great blue-green orb of Earth was becoming visible over the Lunar horizon. Ellen looked at it for a long moment. Then she turned her head to smile mistily at Dall.

"The new home of the Neo-men," she murmured.

Dall's arm tightened about her. "And ours, too, Ellen."

Earth's full orb swelled into view, shining with promise.

THE END

If you've enjoyed this book, you will not want to miss these terrific titles…

ARMCHAIR SCI-FI & HORROR DOUBLE NOVELS, $12.95 each

D-1   **THE GALAXY RAIDERS** by William P. McGivern
       SPACE STATION #1 by Frank Belknap Long

D-2   **THE PROGRAMMED PEOPLE** by Jack Sharkey
       SLAVES OF THE CRYSTAL BRAIN by William Carter Sawtelle

D-3   **YOU'RE ALL ALONE** by Fritz Leiber
       THE LIQUID MAN by Bernard C. Gilford

D-4   **CITADEL OF THE STAR LORDS** by Edmond Hamilton
       VOYAGE TO ETERNITY by Milton Lesser

D-5   **IRON MEN OF VENUS** by Don Wilcox
       THE MAN WITH ABSOLUTE MOTION by Noel Loomis

D-6   **WHO SOWS THE WIND...** by Rog Phillips
       THE PUZZLE PLANET by Robert A. W. Lowndes

D-7   **PLANET OF DREAD** by Murray Leinster
       TWICE UPON A TIME by Charles L. Fontenay

D-8   **THE TERROR OUT OF SPACE** by Dwight V. Swain
       QUEST OF THE GOLDEN APE by Ivar Jorgensen and Adam Chase

D-9   **SECRET OF MARRACOTT DEEP** by Henry Slesar
       PAWN OF THE BLACK FLEET by Mark Clifton.

D-10   **BEYOND THE RINGS OF SATURN** by Robert Moore Williams
       A MAN OBSESSED by Alan E. Nourse

ARMCHAIR SCIENCE FICTION CLASSICS, $12.95 each

C-1   **THE GREEN MAN**
       by Harold M. Sherman

C-2   **A TRACE OF MEMORY**
       By Keith Laumer

C-3   **INTO PLUTONIAN DEPTHS**
       by Stanton A. Coblentz

ARMCHAIR MASTERS OF SCIENCE FICTION SERIES, $16.95 each

M-1   **MASTERS OF SCIENCE FICTION, Vol. One**
       Bryce Walton—"Dark of the Moon" and other tales

M-2   **MASTERS OF SCIENCE FICTION, Vol. Two**
       Jerome Bixby—"One Way Street" and other tales

If you've enjoyed this book, you will not want to miss these terrific titles...

ARMCHAIR SCI-FI & HORROR DOUBLE NOVELS, $12.95 each

D-11 **PERIL OF THE STARMEN** by Kris Neville
THE FORGOTTEN PLANET by Murray Leinster

D-12 **THE STAR LORD** by Boyd Ellanby
CAPTIVES OF THE FLAME by Samuel R. Delany

D-13 **MEN OF THE MORNING STAR** by Edmond Hamilton
PLANET FOR PLUNDER by Hal Clement and Sam Merwin, Jr.

D-14 **ICE CITY OF THE GORGON** by Chester S. Geier and Richard Shaver
WHEN THE WORLD TOTTERED by Lester del Rey

D-15 **WORLDS WITHOUT END** by Clifford D. Simak
THE LAVENDER VINE OF DEATH by Don Wilcox

D-16 **SHADOW ON THE MOON** by Joe Gibson
ARMAGEDDON EARTH by Geoff St. Reynard

D-17 **THE GIRL WHO LOVED DEATH** by Paul W. Fairman
SLAVE PLANET by Laurence M. Janifer

D-18 **SECOND CHANCE** by J. F. Bone
MISSION TO A DISTANT STAR by Frank Belknap Long

D-19 **THE SYNDIC** by C. M. Kornbluth
FLIGHT TO FOREVER by Poul Anderson

D-20 **SOMEWHERE I'LL FIND YOU** by Milton Lesser
THE TIME ARMADA by Fox B. Holden

ARMCHAIR SCIENCE FICTION CLASSICS, $12.95 each

C-4 **CORPUS EARTHLING**
by Louis Charbonneau

C-5 **THE TIME DISSOLVER**
by Jerry Sohl

C-6 **WEST OF THE SUN**
by Edgar Pangborn

ARMCHAIR SCI-FI & HORROR GEMS SERIES, $12.95 each

G-1 **SCIENCE FICTION GEMS, Vol. One**
Isaac Asimov and others

G-2 **HORROR GEMS, Vol. One**
Carl Jacobi and others

If you've enjoyed this book, you will not want to miss these terrific titles…

ARMCHAIR SCI-FI & HORROR DOUBLE NOVELS, $12.95 each

D-21   **EMPIRE OF EVIL** by Robert Arnette
          THE SIGN OF THE TIGER by Alan E. Nourse & J. A. Meyer

D-22   **OPERATION SQUARE PEG** by Frank Belknap Long
          ENCHANTRESS OF VENUS by Leigh Brackett

D-23   **THE LIFE WATCH** by Lester del Rey
          CREATURES OF THE ABYSS by Murray Leinster

D-24   **LEGION OF LAZARUS** by Edmond Hamilton
          STAR HUNTER by Andre Norton

D-25   **EMPIRE OF WOMEN** by John Fletcher
          ONE OF OUR CITIES IS MISSING by Irving Cox

D-26   **THE WRONG SIDE OF PARADISE** by Raymond F. Jones
          THE INVOLUNTARY IMMORTALS by Rog Phillips

D-27   **EARTH QUARTER** by Damon Knight
          ENVOY TO NEW WORLDS by Keith Laumer

D-28   **SLAVES TO THE METAL HORDE** by Milton Lesser
          HUNTERS OUT OF TIME by Joseph E. Kelleam

D-29   **RX JUPITER SAVE US** by Ward Moore
          BEWARE THE USURPERS by Geoff St. Reynard

D-30   **SECRET OF THE SERPENT** by Don Wilcox
          CRUSADE ACROSS THE VOID by Dwight V. Swain

ARMCHAIR SCIENCE FICTION CLASSICS, $12.95 each

C-7   **THE SHAVER MYSTERY, Book One**
        by Richard S. Shaver

C-8   **THE SHAVER MYSTERY, Book Two**
        by Richard S. Shaver

C-9   **MURDER IN SPACE**
        by David V. Reed

ARMCHAIR MASTERS OF SCIENCE FICTION SERIES, $16.95 each

M-3   **MASTERS OF SCIENCE FICTION, Vol. Three**
        Robert Sheckley, "The Perfect Woman" and other tales

M-4   **MASTERS OF SCIENCE FICTION, Vol. Four**
        Mack Reynolds, Part One, "Stowaway" and other tales

If you've enjoyed this book, you will not want to miss these terrific titles…

ARMCHAIR SCI-FI & HORROR DOUBLE NOVELS, $12.95 each

D-31   **A HOAX IN TIME** by Keith Laumer
         INSIDE EARTH by Poul Anderson

D-32   **TERROR STATION** by Dwight V. Swain
         THE WEAPON FROM ETERNITY by Dwight V. Swain

D-33   **THE SHIP FROM INFINITY** by Edmond Hamilton
         TAKEOFF by C. M. Kornbluth

D-34   **THE METAL DOOM** by David H. Keller
         TWELVE TIMES ZERO by Howard Browne

D-35   **HUNTERS OUT OF SPACE** by Joseph Kelleam
         INVASION FROM THE DEEP by Paul W. Fairman,

D-36   **THE BEES OF DEATH** by Robert Moore Williams
         A PLAGUE OF PYTHONS by Frederik Pohl

D-37   **THE LORDS OF QUARMALL** by Fritz Leiber and Harry Fischer
         BEACON TO ELSEWHERE by James H. Schmitz

D-38   **BEYOND PLUTO** by John S. Campbell
         ARTERY OF FIRE by Thomas N. Scortia

D-39   **SPECIAL DELIVERY** by Kris Neville
         NO TIME FOR TOFFEE by Charles F. Meyers

D-40   **JUNGLE IN THE SKY** by Milton Lesser
         RECALLED TO LIFE by Robert Silverberg

ARMCHAIR SCIENCE FICTION CLASSICS, $12.95 each

C-10   **MARS IS MY DESTINATION**
         by Frank Belknap Long

C-11   **SPACE PLAGUE**
         by George O. Smith

C-12   **SO SHALL YE REAP**
         by Rog Phillips

ARMCHAIR SCI-FI & HORROR GEMS SERIES, $12.95 each

G-3   **SCIENCE FICTION GEMS, Vol. Two**
        James Blish and others

G-4   **HORROR GEMS, Vol. Two**
        Joseph Payne Brennan and others

If you've enjoyed this book, you will not want to miss these terrific titles…

ARMCHAIR SCI-FI & HORROR DOUBLE NOVELS, $12.95 each

D-41   **FULL CYCLE** by Clifford D. Simak
    IT WAS THE DAY OF THE ROBOT by Frank Belknap Long

D-42   **THIS CROWDED EARTH** by Robert Bloch
    REIGN OF THE TELEPUPPETS by Daniel Galouye

D-43   **THE CRISPIN AFFAIR** by Jack Sharkey
    THE RED HELL OF JUPITER by Paul Ernst

D-44   **PLANET OF DREAD** by Dwight V. Swain
    WE THE MACHINE by Gerald Vance

D-45   **THE STAR HUNTER** by Edmond Hamilton
    THE ALIEN by Raymond F. Jones

D-46   **WORLD OF IF** by Rog Phillips
    SLAVE RAIDERS FROM MERCURY by Don Wilcox

D-47   **THE ULTIMATE PERIL** by Robert Abernathy
    PLANET OF SHAME by Bruce Elliot

D-48   **THE FLYING EYES** by J. Hunter Holly
    SOME FABULOUS YONDER by Phillip Jose Farmer

D-49   **THE COSMIC BUNGLERS** by Geoff St. Reynard
    THE BUTTONED SKY by Geoff St. Reynard

D-50   **TYRANTS OF TIME** by Milton Lesser
    PARIAH PLANET by Murray Leinster

ARMCHAIR SCIENCE FICTION CLASSICS, $12.95 each

C-13   **SUNKEN WORLD**
    by Stanton A. Coblentz

C-14   **THE LAST VIAL**
    by Sam McClatchie, M. D.

C-15   **WE WHO SURVIVED (THE FIFTH ICE AGE)**
    by Sterling Noel

ARMCHAIR MASTERS OF SCIENCE FICTION SERIES, $16.95 each

MS-5   **MASTERS OF SCIENCE FICTION, Vol. Five**
    Winston K. Marks—Test Colony and other tales

MS-6   **MASTERS OF SCIENCE FICTION, Vol. Six**
    Fritz Leiber—Deadly Moon and other tales

If you've enjoyed this book, you will not want to miss these terrific titles…

ARMCHAIR SCI-FI & HORROR DOUBLE NOVELS, $12.95 each

D-51   **A GOD NAMED SMITH** by Henry Slesar
        WORLDS OF THE IMPERIUM by Keith Laumer

D-52   **CRAIG'S BOOK** by Don Wilcox
        EDGE OF THE KNIFE by H. Beam Piper

D-53   **THE SHINING CITY** by Rena M. Vale
        THE RED PLANET by Russ Winterbotham

D-54   **THE MAN WHO LIVED TWICE** by Rog Phillips
        VALLEY OF THE CROEN by Lee Tarbell

D-55   **OPERATION DISASTER** by Milton Lesser
        LAND OF THE DAMNED by Berkeley Livingston

D-56   **CAPTIVE OF THE CENTAURIANESS** by Poul Anderson
        A PRINCESS OF MARS by Edgar Rice Burroughs

D-57   **THE NON-STATISTICAL MAN** by Raymond F. Jones
        MISSION FROM MARS by Rick Conroy

D-58   **INTRUDERS FROM THE STARS** by Ross Rocklynne
        FLIGHT OF THE STARLING by Chester S. Geier

D-59   **COSMIC SABOTEUR** by Frank M. Robinson
        LOOK TO THE STARS by Willard Hawkins

D-60   **THE MOON IS HELL!** by John W. Campbell, Jr.
        THE GREEN WORLD by Hal Clement

ARMCHAIR SCIENCE FICTION CLASSICS, $12.95 each

C-16   **THE SHAVER MYSTERY, Book Three**
        by Richard S. Shaver

C-17   **THE PLANET STRAPPERS**
        by Raymond Z. Gallun

C-18   **THE FOURTH "R"**
        by George O. Smith

ARMCHAIR SCI-FI & HORROR GEMS SERIES, $12.95 each

G-5   **SCIENCE FICTION GEMS, Vol. Three**
        C. M. Kornbluth and others

G-6   **HORROR GEMS, Vol. Three**
        August Derleth and others

If you've enjoyed this book, you will not want to miss these terrific titles…

ARMCHAIR SCI-FI & HORROR DOUBLE NOVELS, $12.95 each

D-61 **THE MAN WHO STOPPED AT NOTHING** by Paul W. Fairman
TEN FROM INFINITY by Ivar Jorgensen

D-62 **WORLDS WITHIN** by Rog Phillips
THE SLAVE by C.M. Kornbluth

D-63 **SECRET OF THE BLACK PLANET** by Milton Lesser
THE OUTCASTS OF SOLAR III by Emmett McDowell

D-64 **WEB OF THE WORLDS** by Harry Harrison and Katherine MacLean
RULE GOLDEN by Damon Knight

D-65 **TEN TO THE STARS** by Raymond Z. Gallun
THE CONQUERORS by David H. Keller, M. D.

D-66 **THE HORDE FROM INFINITY** by Dwight V. Swain
THE DAY THE EARTH FROZE by Gerald Hatch

D-67 **THE WAR OF THE WORLDS** by H. G. Wells
THE TIME MACHINE by H. G. Wells

D-68 **STARCOMBERS** by Edmond Hamilton
THE YEAR WHEN STARDUST FELL by Raymond F. Jones

D-69 **HOCUS-POCUS UNIVERSE** by Jack Williamson
QUEEN OF THE PANTHER WORLD by Berkeley Livingston

D-70 **BATTERING RAMS OF SPACE** by Don Wilcox
DOOMSDAY WING by George H. Smith

ARMCHAIR SCIENCE FICTION CLASSICS, $12.95 each

C-19 **EMPIRE OF JEGGA**
by David V. Reed

C-20 **THE TOMORROW PEOPLE**
by Judith Merril

C-21 **THE MAN FROM YESTERDAY**
by Howard Browne as by Lee Francis

C-22 **THE TIME TRADERS**
by Andre Norton

C-23 **ISLANDS OF SPACE**
by John W. Campbell

C-24 **THE GALAXY PRIMES**
by E. E. "Doc" Smith

If you've enjoyed this book, you will not want to miss these terrific titles...

ARMCHAIR SCI-FI & HORROR DOUBLE NOVELS, $12.95 each

D-71 **THE DEEP END** by Gregory Luce
TO WATCH BY NIGHT by Robert Moore Williams

D-72 **SWORDSMAN OF LOST TERRA** by Poul Anderson
PLANET OF GHOSTS by David V. Reed

D-73 **MOON OF BATTLE** by J. J. Allerton
THE MUTANT WEAPON by Murray Leinster

D-74 **OLD SPACEMEN NEVER DIE!** John Jakes
RETURN TO EARTH by Bryan Berry

D-75 **THE THING FROM UNDERNEATH** by Milton Lesser
OPERATION INTERSTELLAR by George O. Smith

D-76 **THE BURNING WORLD** by Algis Budrys
FOREVER IS TOO LONG by Chester S. Geier

D-77 **THE COSMIC JUNKMAN** by Rog Phillips
THE ULTIMATE WEAPON by John W. Campbell

D-78 **THE TIES OF EARTH** by James H. Schmitz
CUE FOR QUIET by Thomas L. Sherred

D-79 **SECRET OF THE MARTIANS** by Paul W. Fairman
THE VARIABLE MAN by Philip K. Dick

D-80 **THE GREEN GIRL** by Jack Williamson
THE ROBOT PERIL by Don Wilcox

ARMCHAIR SCIENCE FICTION CLASSICS, $12.95 each

C-25 **THE STAR KINGS**
by Edmond Hamilton

C-26 **NOT IN SOLITUDE**
by Kenneth Gantz

C-32 **PROMETHEUS II**
by S. J. Byrne

ARMCHAIR SCI-FI & HORROR GEMS SERIES, $12.95 each

G-7 **SCIENCE FICTION GEMS, Vol. Four**
Jack Sharkey and others

G-8 **HORROR GEMS, Vol. Four**
Seabury Quinn and others

If you've enjoyed this book, you will not want to miss these terrific titles…

If you've enjoyed this book, you will not want to miss these terrific titles…